Tom Swift in the Caves of Ice

Victor Appleton

Contents

TOM SWIFT IN THE CAVES OF ICE

BY

Victor Appleton

CHAPTER I
ERADICATE IN AN AIRSHIP

Well, Massa Tom, am yo' gwine out in yo' flyin' machine ag'in to-day?"

"Yes, Rad, I think I will take a little flight. Perhaps I'll go over to Waterford, and call on Mr. Damon. I haven't seen very much of him, since we got back from our hunt after the diamond-makers."

"Take a run clear ober t' Waterfield; eh, Massa Tom?"

"Yes, Rad. Now, if you'll help me, I'll get out the Butterfly, and see what trim she's in for a speedy flight."

Tom Swift, the young inventor, aided by Eradicate Sampson, the colored helper of the Swift household, walked over toward a small shed.

A few minutes later the two had rolled into view, on its three bicycle wheels, a trim little monoplane--one of the speediest craft of the air that had ever skimmed along beneath the clouds. It was built to carry two, and had a very powerful motor.

"I guess it will work all right," remarked the young inventor, for Torn Swift had not only built this monoplane himself, but was the originator of it, and the craft contained many new features.

"It sho' do look all right, Massa Tom."

"Look here, Rad," spoke the lad, as a sudden idea came to him, "you've never ridden in an airship, have you?"

"No, Massa Tom, an' I ain't gwine to nuther!"

"Why not?"

"Why not? 'Case as how it ain't healthy; that's why!"

"But I go in them frequently, Eradicate. So does my father. You've seen us fly often enough, to know that it's safe. Why, look at the number of times Mr. Damon and I have gone off on trips in this little Butterfly. Didn't we always come back safely?"

"Yes, dat's true, but dere might come a time when yo' WOULDN'T come back, an' den where'd Eradicate Sampson be? I axes yo' dat--whar'd I be, Massa Tom?"

"Why, you wouldn't be anywhere if you didn't go, of course," and Tom laughed. "But I'd like to take you for a little spin in this machine, Rad. I want you to get used to them. Sometime I may need you to help me. Come, now. Suppose you get up on this seat here, and I promise not to go too high until you get used to it. Come on, it will do you good, and think of what all your friends will say when they see you riding in an airship."

"Dat's right, Massa Tom. Dey suah will be monstrous envious ob Eradicate Sampson, dat's what dey will."

It was clear that the colored man was being pursuaded somewhat against his will. Though he had been engaged by Tom Swift and his father off and on for several years, Eradicate had never shown any desire to take a trip through the air in one of the several craft Tom owned for this purpose. Nor had he ever evinced a longing for a trip under the ocean in a submarine, and as for riding in Tom's speedy electric car--Eradicate would as soon have sat down with thirteen at the table, or looked at the moon over the wrong shoulder.

But now, somehow, there was a peculiar temptation to take his young employer at his word. Eradicate had seen, many times, the youthful inventor and his friends make trips in the monoplane, as well as in the big biplane and dirigible balloon combined--the RED CLOUD. Tom and the others had always come back safely, though often they met with accidents which only the skill and daring of the daring aeronaut had brought to a safe conclusion.

"Well, are you coming, Rad?" asked Tom, as he looked to see if the oil and gasoline tanks were filled, and gave a preliminary twirl to the propeller.

"Now does yo' t'ink it am puffickly safe, Massa Tom?" and the colored man looked nervously at the machine.

"Of course, Rad. Otherwise I wouldn't invite you. But I won't take you far. I just want you to get used to it, and, once you have made a flight, you'll want to make another."

"I don't nohow believe I will, Massa Tom, but as long as you have axed me, an' as yo' say some of dem proud, stuck-up darkies in Shopton will be tooken down a peg or two when de sees me, vhy, I will go wif yo', Massa Tom."

"I thought you would. Now take your place in the little seat next to where I'm going to sit. All start the engine and jump in. Now sit perfectly still, and, whatever you do, don't jump out. The ground's pretty hard this morning. There was a frost last night."

"I knows dere was, Massa Tom. Nope, I won't jump. I-I-Oh, golly, Massa Tom! I guess I don't want to go-let me out!"

Eradicate, his heart growing fainter as the time of starting drew nearer, made as if he would leave the monoplane, in which he had taken his seat.

"Sit still!" yelled Tom. At that instant he started the propeller. The motor roared like a salvo of guns, and streaks of fire could be seen shooting from one cylinder to the other, until there was a perfect blast of explosions.

The speed of the propeller increased as the motor warmed up. Tom ran to his seat and opened the gasoline throttle still more, advancing the spark slightly. The roar increased. The lad darted a look at Eradicate. The colored man's face was like chalk, and he was gripping the upright braces at his side as though his salvation depended on them.

"Steady now" spoke Tom, yelling to be heard above the racket. "Here we go."

The Butter-fly was moving slowly across the level stretch of ground which Tom used for starting his airships. The propeller was now a blur of light. The explosions of the motor became a steady roar, the noise from one cylinder being merged into the blast from the others so rapidly that it was a continuous racket.

With a whizz the monoplane shot across the ground. Then, with a quick motion, Tom tilted the lifting planes, and, as gracefully as a bird, the little machine mounted upward on a slant until, coming to a level about two hundred feet above the earth, Tom sent it straight ahead over the roof of his house.

"How's this, Rad?" he cried. "Isn't it great?"

"It--it--er--bur-r-r-r! It's--it's mighty ticklish, Massa Tom-dat's de word--it suah am mighty ticklish!"

Tom Swift laughed and increased the speed. The Butterfly darted forward like some hummingbird about to launch itself upon a flower, and, indeed, the revolutions of the propeller were not unlike the vibrations of the wings of that marvelous little creature.

"Now for some corkscrew twists!" cried the young inventor. "Here we go, Rad!"

With that he began a series of intricate evolutions, making figures of eight, spirals, curves, sudden dips and long swings. It was masterwork in handling a monoplane, but Eradicate Sampson, as he sat crouched in the seat, gripping the uprights until his hands ached, was in no condition to appreciate it. Gradually, however, as he saw that the craft remained up in the air, and showed no signs of falling, the fears of the colored man left him. He sat up straighter.

"Don't you like it, Rad?" cried Tom.

This time the answer came with more decision.

"It suah am great, Massa Tom! I'm--I'm beginnin' t' like it. Whoop! I guess I do like it! Now if some of dem stuck-up coons could see me--"

"They'd think YOU were stuck up; eh, Rad? Stuck up in the air!"

"Dat's right, Massa Tom. Ha! Ha! I suah am stuck up in de air! Ha! Ha!"

By this time Tom had guided the machine away from the village, and they were flying over the fields, some distance from his house. The colored man was beginning to enjoy his experience very much.

Suddenly, just as Tom was trying to get a bit more speed out of the motor, the machine stopped. The cessation of the racket was almost as startling as a loud explosion would have been.

"Just my luck!" cried Tom.

"What's de matter?" asked Eradicate, anxiously.

"Motor's stalled," replied the young inventor.

"An', by golly, we's falling!" yelled the colored man.

Naturally, with the stopping of the propeller, there was no further straight, forward motion to the monoplane, and, following the law of nature, it began to drop toward the earth on a slant.

"We's fallin'! We'll be killed!" yelled the negro.

"It's all right, I'll just vol-plane back to earth," spoke Tom, calmly. "I've often done it before, higher up than this. Sit still, Rad, I'm volplaning back to the ground."

"An' I'll JUMP back to de ground; dat's what I'll do. I ain't goin' t' wait until I falls, no sah! An' I ain't gwine t' do none ob dat ball-playin' yo' speak ob, Massa Swift. It's no time t' play ball when yo' life am in danger. I'se gwine t' jump."

"Sit still!" cried Tom, for the colored man was about to spring from his seat. "There's no danger! I didn't say anything about playing ball. I said I'd VOL-PLANE back to the earth. We'll be there shortly. I'll take you down safe. Sit still, Rad!"

He spoke so earnestly that the fears of his colored passenger were quelled. With a quick motion Tom threw up the head planes, to check the downward sweep. The Butterfly shot forward on a gradual slant. Repeating this maneuver several times, the young inventor finally brought his machine to within a short distance of the earth, and, also, considerably nearer his own home.

"I wonder if we can make it?" he murmured, measuring the distance with his eye. "I think so. I'll shoot her up a bit and then let her down on a long slant. Then, with another upward tilt, I ought to fetch it."

The monoplane tilted upward. Eradicate gave a cry of terror. It was stilled at a look from Tom. Once more the air machine glided forward. Then came another long dip, another upward glide and the Butterfly came gently to earth almost on the very spot whence it had flown upward a few minutes before.

Eradicate gave one mad spring from his seat, almost before the bicycle wheels had ceased revolving, as Tom jammed on the earth-brake.

"Here, where are you going, Rad?" cried the lad.

"Whar am I goin'? I'se goin' t' see if mah mule Boomerang am safe. He's de only kind ob an airship I wants arter dis!" and the colored man disappeared into the shack whence came a loud "hee-haw!"

"Oh, pshaw! Wait a minute, Rad. I'll soon have the motor fixed, and we'll make another try. I'll take you over to Mr. Damon's with me."

"No, sah, Massa Tom. Yo' don't catch dis coon in any mo' airships. Mah mule am good enough fo' me!" shouted Eradicate from the safe harbor of the mule's stable.

Tom laughed, and turned to inspect the motor. As he was looking it over, to locate the trouble, the door of the house opened and a pleasant-faced woman stepped out.

"Oh, Tom," she called. "I looked for you a moment ago, and you weren't here!"

"No, Mrs. Baggert," Tom replied, waving his hand in greeting to the housekeeper, "Rad and I just came back--quite suddenly--sooner than we expected to. Why? Did you want me?"

"Here's a letter that came for you," she went on.

Tom tore open the envelope, and rapidly scanned the contents of the missive.

"Hello!" he ejaculated half aloud. "It's from Abe Abercrombie, that miner I met when we were after the diamond-makers! He says he is on his way east to get ready to start on the quest for the Alaskan valley of gold, in the caves of ice. I had almost forgotten that I promised to make the attempt in the big airship. How did this letter come, Mrs. Baggert?" he asked.

"By special delivery. The messenger brought it a few minutes ago."

"Then we may see Abe any day now. Guess I'd better be looking over the RED CLOUD to see if it's in shape for a trip to the Arctic regions."

Tom's attention for the moment was taken off his little monoplane, and his memory went back to the strange scenes in which he and his friends had recently played a part, in searching for the cave of the diamond-makers on Phantom Mountain. He recalled the promise he had made to the old miner.

"I wonder if he expects us to start for Alaska with winter coming on?" thought Tom. His musings were suddenly interrupted by the entrance into the yard, surrounding the aeroplane shed, of a lad about his own age.

"Hello, Ned Newton!" called Tom, heartily.

"Hello, yourself," responded Ned. "I've got a day off from the bank, and I thought I'd come over and see you. Say, have you heard the latest?"

"No. What is it?"

"Andy Foger is building an airship."

"Andy Foger building an airship?"

"Yes, he says it will beat yours."

"Humph! It will, eh? Well, Andy can do as he pleases as long as he doesn't bother me. I won't be around here much longer, anyhow."

"Why not, Tom?"

"Because I soon expect to start for the far north on a strange quest. Come on in the shed, and I'll tell you about it. We're going to try to locate a valley of gold, and I guess Andy Foger won't follow me there, even if he does build an airship."

Tom and his chum started toward the shed, the young inventor still holding the letter that was to play such an important part in his life within the next few months. And, had he only known it, the building of Andy Foger's airship was destined to be fraught with much danger to our hero.

CHAPTER II
ANDY FOGER'S TRIPLANE

G oing to look for a valley of gold, eh?" remarked Ned Newton as he and Tom took seats in a little room, fitted up like a den, where the young inventor frequently worked out the details of the problems that confronted him. "Where is this valley, Tom? Anywhere so I could have a chance at it?"

"It's up in Alaska. Just where I don't know, but Abe Abercrombie, the old miner whom we met when out in Colorado this summer, says he can find it if we circle around in the airship. So I'm going to take a chance. I'll tell you all about it."

And, while Tom is doing this, I will take the opportunity to more formally introduce to my new readers our hero and his friends.

Tom Swift was an inventor of no little note, in spite of his youth. He lived with his father, Barton Swift, who was also an inventor, on the outskirts of the village of Shopton, New York State. Tom's mother was dead, and Mrs. Baggert had kept house for him and his father since he was a child. Garret Jackson, an expert machinist, was also a member of the household, and as has been explained, Eradicate Sampson, who took that name because, as he said he "eradicate de dirt," was also a sort of retainer. He lived in a little house on the Swift grounds, and did odd jobs about the place.

In the first book of the series, entitled "Tom Swift and His Motor Cycle," there was related how the lad became possessed of one of those speedy machines, after Mr. Wakefield Damon had come to grief on it. Mr. Damon was an eccentric man, who was always blessing himself, some part of his anatomy, or some of his possessions.

After many adventures on his motor-cycle, Tom Swift went through some surprising happenings with a motor-boat be bought. After that he built an airship, the RED CLOUD, and later he and his father constructed a submarine, in which they went under the ocean in search of sunken treasure, enduring many perils and much danger.

Tom Swift's electric runabout, which he built after returning home from the submarine trip, proved to be the speediest car on the road. The experience he acquired in making this machine stood him in good stead, when (as told in the sixth volume, "Tom Swift and His Wireless Message") the airship in which he, Mr. Damon and a friend of the latter's (who had built the craft) were wrecked on Earthquake Island. There Tom was marooned with some refugees from a wrecked steam yacht, among whom were Mr. and Mrs. Nestor, father of a girl of whom Tom thought a great deal.

With parts from the wrecked electric airship the youth rigged up a plant, and sent wireless messages from the island. The castaways nearly lost their lives in the earthquake shocks, but a steamer, summoned by Tom's wireless call, arrived in time to save them, just as the island disappeared beneath the sea.

In the seventh book of the series, entitled "Tom Swift Among the Diamond Makers" there was related the adventures of himself and his friends when they tried to solve the mystery of Phantom Mountain.

Among the castaways of Earthquake Island was a Mr. Barcoe Jenks and a Professor Ralph Parker. Mr. Jenks was a strange man, and claimed to have some valuable diamonds, which he said were made by a gang of men hidden in a cave in the Rocky Mountains. Tom did not believe that the diamonds were real, but Mr. Jenks soon proved that they were.

He asked Tom to aid him in searching for the cave of the diamond makers. Mr. Jenks had been there once--in fact, he had been offered a partnership in the diamond-making business, but, after he had paid his money, he had been drugged, and carried secretly from the cave before he had a chance to note its location.

But he, together with Tom, Mr. Damon and the scientist Mr. Parker, who correctly predicted the destruction of Earthquake Island, set out in the RED CLOUD to find the diamond makers. They did find them, after many hardships, and were captured by the gang. How Tom and his friends escaped from the cave, after they had seen diamonds made by a powerful lightning flash, and how they nearly lost their lives from the destruction of Phantom Mountain, is fully set down in the book.

Sufficient to say now, that, though they had a general idea of how the precious stones were made, by the power of the lightning, the young inventor and his friends were never quite able to accomplish it, and the secret remained a secret. But they had secured some diamonds as they rushed from the cave (Mr. Damon grabbing them up) and these were divided among Tom and the others.

Just as they were ready to come home in the airship, our friends were met by an old miner, Abe Abercrombie, who spoke of a valley of gold in Alaska, which was the story Tom related to Ned Newton, as the two chums sat in the den of the airship shed.

"Then you don't know all the details about the gold valley, Tom?" remarked Ned, as the young inventor showed his chum the letter that had just arrived.

"No, not all of them. At the time this miner met us I was anxious to get back East, for we had been away so long I knew dad would be worried. But I listened to part of Abe's story, and half promised to go in partnership in this quest for gold. He was to furnish information about the hidden valley, and I was to supply the airship. I expect Abe to come along at any time, now, and then I'll hear more particulars."

"Will you go all the way in the airship?"

"Well, I hadn't thought of that. I could ship it to the nearest place by rail, I suppose, and go on from there. That's a detail to be considered later. I'll talk it over with Abe."

"Who are going?"

"I don't know that even. I suppose Mr. Damon would feel slighted if I left him out. And perhaps Mr. Parker, that gloomy scientist, who is always predicting terrible accidents, will be glad to go along. Then Abe may have some friend he wants to take."

"By Jinks! But you certainly do have swell times, Tom Swift!" exclaimed Ned Newton, enviously. "I wish I could go and have a try at that valley of gold!"

"Why don't you come along, Ned?"

"Do you really mean it?"

"Of course."

"But I don't believe I could get away from the bank."

"Oh, dad and Mr. Damon could fix that. They're directors, you know. Come along, I'd be delighted to have you. Will you?"

"I'll think about it. Jinks! But I sure would like to go. Do you think you can find the valley?"

"Well, there's no telling. We generally do succeed in finding what we go after, even if we didn't get the diamond secret. I'm anxious to have Abe come, now, though until I got his letter I had almost forgotten about my promise to him. But, say, what's this you told me about Andy Foger making an airship?"

"It's true, though I haven't seen it. Jake Porter was telling me about it. Andy's built a big shed in his yard, and he and some cronies of his, including Pete Bailey and Sam Snedecker, are working in there night and day. They've hired a couple of machinists, too. Mr. Foger is putting up the cash, I guess. Say, that was quite a scare you gave Andy on your monoplane, one day."

"Yes, the big bully! and I'd like to scare him worse. But say, do you know I'd like to get a look at his airship. I wonder what sort of a craft it is?"

"We can see it easily enough."

"How?"

"Why, the back part of the shed where he and the others are working is close to our fence. There are some holes in our fence and if you come there, maybe you can look in."

"I can't see through the side of the shed, though."

"Yes, you can."

"How?"

"Why, there's a big window, for light, in the back part of it. I happened to notice it the other day. I didn't look in, because I wasn't much interested, but I saw that one could peer over the top of our fence right into the shop where Andy is working. Want to try it?"

Tom hesitated a moment.

"Well, it seems rather an odd thing to do," he said. "But I would like to see what sort of a flying machine Andy is making, just for my own satisfaction. He may be infringing on some of my patents, and if he is, I'll stop him. Once or twice he's been sneaking around my shed here. I don't believe in sneaking, but I know he wouldn't let me in if I asked him, so I guess it's the only way. I'll go with you, Ned."

"All right. We'll see if we can get a glimpse of Andy's queer shebang through the window."

The two chums left Tom's shop, and were soon in the yard of Ned Newton's house. As he had said, the big shed in Andy's premises came close up to the fence, and there was a window through which one might gaze. The casement did not appear to be curtained.

"I'll get a ladder so we can climb up to the top of the fence, and look over," spoke Ned, as he and Tom went out into the yard back of his house. The fence was high up on an embankment.

A little later Tom and his chum were gazing into the shop window from the ladder.

"Why, it's a triplane--a big triplane!" he exclaimed.

"What's a triplane?" asked Ned, who didn't have much time to study the different types of airships.

"It's one that has three sets of planes, one above the other. A biplane has two sets of planes, and a monoplane only one. Triplanes are larger, and, as far as I've been able to learn, not as satisfactory as either the biplanes or monoplanes. But that's not saying Andy's won't be a success. They certainly are busy in there, though! Andy is flying around like a hen scratching for her little chickens!"

"See anything of his cronies?"

"Yes, Pete and Sam are hammering away. There are a couple of men, too."

"Yes, the machinists. Oh, I guess Andy expects great things from his airship."

"Have you heard what he's going to do with it, Ned? Make flights for pleasure, or exhibit it?"

"No, I haven't heard. Look out, Tom, the ladder is slipping!"

As Ned spoke this warning, the window of the airship shed, through which they were looking, was suddenly raised. The ugly face of Andy Foger peered out. He caught sight of Tom and Ned.

"Get away from there, you spies!" he yelled. "Get away from there, Tom Swift! You're trying to steal some of my ideas! Get away or I'll make you. Sam, bring me my gun! Pete, go tell my father to come here! I'll show Ned Newton and Tom Swift they can't bother me!"

Andy was dancing about in a rage. His two cronies crowded behind him to the window just as the ladder on which Tom and Ned were standing slipped along the fence.

"Jump, Ned!" yelled Tom Swift, as he leaped away to escape being entangled in the rungs.

The young inventor came to the ground with a jar that shook him up considerably, while Ned, who had grasped the top board of the fence, remained hanging there by his hands, his feet dangling in the air.

"Whack his fingers, Andy!" yelled Pete Bailey. "Get a long stick and whack Ned's fingers! That will make him drop off!"

Tom Swift heard, and labored desperately to raise the ladder to enable Ned to get down, for his chum seemed to be afraid to drop.

CHAPTER III
ABE IS DECEIVED

Raising a ladder alone is rather an awkward job. Tom found this so when he tried to aid his friend Ned. But, being a muscular lad, the young inventor did finally succeed in getting the ladder up against the fence where the bank clerk could reach it.

Whack! Down upon the top board came a stick wielded by Andy Foger from the rear window of his shop.

"Wow!" cried Ned, for the blow had been close to his fingers. "Hurry up with that ladder, Tom."

"There it is! But why don't you drop?"

"Too far. I can't reach the ladder now!"

"Yes, you can. Stretch a bit!"

"Whack!" Once more the stick descended on the fence, this time still closer to Ned's clinging hands.

"Hit him good, Andy!" cried Sam Snedecker, "Give me a shot at him!"

"I will not. I want to attend to him myself. You go tell my father, and he'll have Tom Swift arrested for trying to sneak in and get some of my airship ideas!"

By this time Ned's wiggling feet had found the topmost rung of the ladder. The next moment he was rapidly descending it, and, when on the ground, he and Tom carried it away, to prevent its use by the enemy.

"Whew!" exclaimed the young inventor. "I had no idea they would kick up such a row!"

"Me either. Did you hurt yourself when you jumped, as the ladder fell?"

"No. Did they hit your hands?"

"Came mighty near it. Well, I s'pose it serves us right, yet if I can't look over my own back fence it's a pity!"

"Of course we can, only I'd just as soon they hadn't seen us. However--hello! there's Andy looking over here, now."

The mean face of the bully now topped the fence. It was evident that he had crawled from the window of his shop.

"What are you trying to get into my place for, Tom Swift?" he demanded.

"I wasn't trying to get in, Andy Foger."

"Well, you were looking in."

"Only doing as you've done over at my shop, several times, Andy. I wanted to see what sort of an airship you were building."

"Trying to get some ideas for your own, I guess," sneered Andy.

Tom did not think it worth while to answer this taunt.

"I could have you arrested for this," went on Andy, who felt bolder now that he was reinforced by Sam and Pete on either side of him as he looked over the fence into Ned's yard.

"Arrested for what?" demanded the bank clerk.

"For trespassing on my father's premises," went on Andy.

"We weren't on your premises," declared Ned. "We were on our side of the fence all the while."

"Well, you were looking over in my yard."

"A cat may look at a king, you know, Andy," Tom reminded the bully.

"Yah! Think you're smart, don't you! Well, you can't steal any of my ideas for an airship. They're all patented, and I'll soon be making longer and higher flights than you ever dreamed of! I'll show you what a real airship is, Tom Swift! Monoplanes and biplanes are out of date. The only thing that's any good is a triplane. If mine works well--and I'm sure it will--I may build a quadruplane!"

"I wish you luck," spoke Tom, with a shrug of his shoulders.

"Well, you won't have any luck if you come around here any more," went on Pete Bailey. "We'll be on the watch for you fellows, now, and we'll cover this window, so you can't see in."

"That's what we will," agreed Andy, and Sam Snedecker shook his head vigorously to indicate that he, too, approved of this.

"Come on," spoke Tom in a low tone to Ned, "I've seen enough."

The two chums moved toward Ned's house, followed by the jeers and mocking laughter of Andy and his cronies.

"Can't you get back at them in some way?" asked Ned, for he did not like to see himself or his friend apparently vanquished by the bully.

"He laughs best who laughs last, Ned."

"What do you mean?"

"I mean that when Andy tries to fly in his triplane it will be our turn to laugh."

"Won't it fly?"

"Never, the way he has it rigged up. It didn't take but one look to tell me that. He's working on altogether the wrong principle. Wait until he tries to go up, and then we'll have some fun with him."

"Then you got a good view of it through the window?"

"I saw all I wanted to. But say, I was about to take a little trip in my monoplane, to see my friend Mr. Damon, when Abe's letter arrived, and you came along with your news. I started to take Eradicate, but he backed out. Don't you want to come?"

"Sure, I'll go along."

Ned had often ridden in the trim Butterfly, though the trips had not been so frequent that he was tired of them. A little later, Tom, having adjusted the motor that had stalled before, compelling him to vol-plane back to earth, the two chums were sailing through the air toward Waterford.

"Why, bless my shoe laces!" cried Mr. Damon, as they alighted in the yard of his house, about an hour later. "I didn't expect you, Tom. But I'm glad to see you!"

"And I to meet you again. I guess you know Ned Newton."

"Ah, yes. How d'ye do, Ned? Bless my appetite! but it's quite chilly. We'll soon have winter. Won't you come in and have some hot chocolate?"

The boys were glad to accept the invitation, and as they were drinking the beverage, which Mrs. Damon made for them, Tom told of the receipt of the letter from the old miner, and also his experience in seeing Andy's airship.

"Why, bless my pocketbook!" cried Mr. Damon. "I had no idea we'd ever hear from Abe Abercrombie again. And so he is really coming on, to tell us about the valley of gold?"

"So he says," replied Tom. "I was wondering if you'd like to go, Mr. Damon."

"Go? Why, bless my very topknot! Of course I would. I'll go with you--only--

only," and he leaned forward and whispered cautiously, "don't speak so loudly. My wife might hear you!"

"Doesn't she want you to go off in the airship any more?" asked Tom.

"Well, she'd rather I wouldn't. But she's going on a visit to her mother, soon, and then I think will come my opportunity to take another trip with you. A valley of gold in Alaska, eh? Up where the icebergs and caves of ice are. Say, Tom, I know some one else who would be glad to go."

"Who?" inquired the young inventor, though he had an idea to whom his friend referred.

"Mr. Parker! You know he's taken up his residence in Waterford, now, and only the other day he spoke to me about wishing he could go to the far north. He has some new theory--"

"About the destruction of something or other; hasn't he, Mr. Damon?" interrupted Tom, with a smile.

"That's it, exactly, my boy. Bless my coffeepot! But Mr. Parker has an idea that the whole northern part of this continent will soon be buried thousands of feet deep under an icy avalanche, and he wants to be there to see it. I know he'd like to go with us, Tom."

The young inventor made a little gesture of dissent, but as he knew Mr. Damon, who was very eccentric himself, had taken a great liking to the gloomy scientist, Tom did not feel like refusing. So he said:

"All right, Mr. Damon. If we go, and I think we shall, we'll expect you and Mr. Parker. I'll let you know the result of Mr. Abercrombie's visit, and I needn't request you to keep quiet about it. If there is a valley of gold in Alaska, we don't want everyone to know about it."

"No, of course not, Tom Swift. I'll keep silent about it. Bless my liverpin! But I'll be glad to on the move again, even if it is toward the Arctic regions."

After some further talk, Tom and Ned took their departure, making good time back to Shopton in the speedy monoplane.

For several days after that Tom busied himself about his big airship the RED CLOUD, for it needed quite a few repairs after the long trip to the mountains where the diamond makers had been discovered in their cave.

"And if we're going up amid the ice and snow," reasoned Tom, "I've got to make some different arrangements about the craft, and provide for keeping warmer than we found necessary when we went west."

So it was that Tom had no time to learn anything further about Andy Foger's airship, even had our hero been so inclined, which he was not. He looked for Abe Abercrombie any day now, for though the old miner had given no date as to when he would arrive, he had said, in his letter, that it would be soon.

It was one day, nearly a week after Tom's attempt to make Eradicate like aeroplaning, that there might have been seen, coming along the Shopton road, which led toward Tom's house, the figure of a grizzled old man. His clothes were rather rough, and he carried a valise that had, evidently, seen much service. There was that about him which proclaimed him for a westerner--a cattleman or a miner.

He walked slowly along, murmuring to himself.

"Wa'al, I might better have taken one of them wagons at th' depot," he said, "than t' try t' walk. It's quite a stretch out t' Tom Swift's house. I hope I find him home."

He trudged on, and, a little later, his gaze was attracted by a large shed, in the rear of a white house the pretentious appearance of which indicated that persons of wealth owned it.

"I guess that must be the place," he remarked. "That shed is big enough to hold the airship. Now to present myself."

As he walked up the front path of the house, he was met by one of the gardeners, who was raking up the leaves.

"Is this the airship place?" asked the miner.

"Yes, that's where the young master is making his triplane," answered the man.

"Is he in?"

"Yes, I guess so. You can walk right back to the shed."

The miner did so. Through the open door of the building he had a glimpse of big stretches of wings, propellers, rudders, and some machinery.

"That's it," he murmured, "though it looks some different than I remembered it. However, maybe Tom's changed it about. I wonder where he is?"

As he spoke a lad came from the shed to meet him--a lad on whose face there was a look of suspicion.

"What do you want?" he demanded.

"I'm lookin' for Tom Swift," was the simple reply. "But I take it you're one of his partners in this airship business. I guess he must have told you about me. I'm Abe Abercrombie, the miner, and I've come to show him the way to that valley of gold in Alaska."

At the mention of Tom Swift's name, Andy Foger, for it was he, had started to utter a denial. But, at the next words of the miner, and as Mr. Abercrombie mentioned "gold" and "Alaska," there came a cunning look over Andy's face.

"Tom Swift isn't here just now," he said, wondering how he could turn to advantage the unexpected visit, and the impending information that the guileless old man was about to give under the mistaken idea that Andy was Tom's friend.

"That's all right, I reckon he'll be along presently. You'll do just as well, I reckon. You're in partnership with him, I take it. So this is the place where he makes his airships, eh? It's a big one," and Mr. Abercrombie looked in at the odd triplane of Andy's--for the airship was almost finished.

"But it'll need to be big if we're to go to Alaska in it," went on the miner. "It's quite a journey t' th' valley where th' gold is. No way t' get t' it except by an airship. An' here I be an' ready to start, I've brought th' map of th' place, jest as I promised. Here it is, better take good care of it. Now, let's talk business," and the miner, having guilelessly handed Andy Foger a folded parchment, sat down on a box at the door of the airship shed, and placed his heavy valise on the ground beside him.

"What's this?" asked the bully, wondering whether he had heard aright.

"It's the map of th' valley of gold--directions how t' git there, an' all that. I guess it's plain enough. Now, when can we start?"

Andy did not know what to say. Fate had, most unexpectedly, placed in his hands a valuable paper. The miner had made a mistake. Andy's house was on the same road as was Tom's and, seeing the airship shed, had deceived the aged man. He had not expected to find two airship manufactories in the same village.

"The map of the valley of gold," murmured Andy, as he put it in his pocket.

"Yes, jest as I told Tom about when I met him out West. I said I'd bring it with me, an' I did. When will Tom be back? He never spoke of you, though I reckoned he'd have to have some help in makin' his airships. Where is he?"

"He--he--" stammered Andy. He did not know what to say.

At that instant Tom Swift himself passed by in the road. He had been over to

Shopton on an errand. One look into the yard of Andy's house showed to our hero the old miner sitting at the door of the airship shed.

"Mr. Abercrombie--Abe!" cried Tom, almost, before he thought.

"Hello, Tom! I got here!" cried the miner, heartily. "I was jest talking to your partner."

"My partner!" spoke Tom in amazement

"Yes--partner in th' airship business. I should think you'd need about three partners to build these machines!"

"My partner! Andy Foger isn't my partner!" cried Tom, wondering what would happen next. "I have no partner! If he said he was he deceived you!"

"No partner? Ain't he your partner?" cried Mr. Abercrombie. "Why, I thought he was. I told him about th' valley of gold--I--I--give him the map--"

"The map?"

"Yes, the map t' tell how to get there. He's got it!"

There was a mocking smile on Andy's face.

"Give that map back at once!" cried Tom, sternly, now understanding something of the situation. "Hand it over at once, Andy Foger!"

"I will--when I get ready! He gave it to me!" cried the bully, and then, before either Tom or Abe could stop him, Andy darted into the big shed, and slammed shut the door.

CHAPTER IV
TOM GETS THE MAP

For a few seconds Tom was so surprised at the sudden action of the bully that he could neither move nor speak. Then, crying out a command to halt, the young inventor took after his enemy.

"The scamp!" he cried. "The nerve he has! To deceive Abe Abercrombie in that fashion! Wait until I get hold of him!"

"What's it all about?" asked the old miner, who, being a slow thinker had not understood all that had happened. "What's up, Tom Swift?"

"Haven't time to tell you now," flung back the running lad over his shoulder. "I've got to catch Andy! Then I'll explain. He's trying to get ahead of us. I guess, but we'll stop him!" Thereupon Tom flung himself against the door of the airship shed. The young inventor found the portal bolted, though it vibrated with the impact of his body.

"Come out of there, Andy Foger!" cried Tom, pounding on the door. "Come out, or I'll get an officer, and have you arrested!"

There was no answer.

"Come out, I say!" repeated Tom.

"Around th' back! Try th' back door!" suggested the miner, who had hastened to Tom's side. "Maybe he's run out that way!"

Tom listened. There was no movement in the shop. Then the young inventor sprinted around the side. He was just in time to see the bully running away over the lots and fields in the rear of his father's premises. Andy had climbed out of the back window of the shed, into which Tom and Ned had peered that day, had climbed the high fence, dropped down on the other side, and was now running away with all the speed he could muster.

"Come back--!" began Tom, and then he realized that his enemy could not hear him. The bully was too far away. At the same time our hero realized that it would be useless to give chase, for Andy had too much of a start. There was nothing to do but to turn back, and Tom knew that his delay in trying to gain an entrance at the front door had given Andy the very opportunity he needed to escape at the rear.

"Well, this is a bad turn of affairs," remarked the lad, as he faced the puzzled miner.

"What is, Tom?"

"Him having that map. It shows the location of the valley of gold, doesn't it, and tells how to get there?"

"That's what it does!"

"How did Andy happen to get it?"

"Jest as I told you. I was on my way t' your house, havin' inquired at th' post-office, an' the man said that at your place there was a big shed, where you kept your airships. I come along, an', of course, when I see this house, an' the shed, an' had a glimpse of th' airship, I, of course, thought it was your place. An', though you'd never told me about it, I thought maybe this lad was in business with you. So, like a blamed young tenderfoot, I blurted out my business afore I thought, an' handed him the map for safe keepin'. He took it, too, that's the worst of it."

"Yes, that's the worst of it," agreed Tom, "But I'll get it back, if I have to cause his arrest, and search his whole house."

"But he runned away, Tom."

"Oh, he'll come back. Was there only one copy of the map of the valley, Abe?" asked Tom, anxiously.

"Yep; only one."

"Could you make another?"

"No, not if you was to pay me a million dollars! You see I ain't no drawer, an' this map, while I made part of it, was mostly made by my old partner, who was with me when we discovered th' valley of gold, an' was druv back by th' savage Eskimos an' Indians, an' by th' terrible cold. My partner made th' best part of th' map, an' he's dead, poor fellow."

"I see. That's too bad! Then you can't make a duplicate map?"

"Nary a one. But can't you do somethin'? It were amazin' stupid of me, old Abe

Abercrombie, t' be took in by a boy like him! Can't you do somethin'?"

"I'm going to try," announced Tom determinedly, as he swung on toward the Foger house. "I'll cause his arrest if he doesn't give it up."

A few minutes later Tom Swift and Abe confronted Mr. Foger. The rich man, father of the bully, was rather surprised at the visit from the young inventor, for the two were not friends.

"Well, what can I do for you, Tom Swift?" asked the banker, for he felt a certain coldness toward our hero, since the latter had defeated him in an effort to wreck a financial institution in which Tom and his father were interested.

"Mr. Foger," spoke Tom, sternly, "your son has just stolen a map belonging to this gentleman," and he indicated Abe.

"My son stolen a map!" exclaimed Mr. Foger. "How dare you make such an accusation, Tom Swift?"

"I dare, because it's true! And, unless that map is returned to me at my house to-night I shall swear out a warrant for Andy's arrest."

"You'd never dare do that!"

"Wait and see!" spoke Tom, firmly. "I will give your son, or you, exactly five hours to return that map--if it isn't back in my hands by then, I'll get a warrant!"

"Preposterous! Stuff and nonsense!" blustered Mr. Foger. "My son never stole anything!"

"He stole this map, and there is plenty of evidence," went on Tom, as he detailed the circumstances.

Mr. Foger hemmed and hawed, and affected not to believe that anything of the kind could have happened. But Tom was firm, and Abe Abercrombie backed up his statements, until even the banker began to waver.

"Very well," he announced at length, "I will look into this matter, and if I find that my son has anything of yours, you shall have it back. But I cannot believe it. Perhaps he took it as a joke."

"In which case," spoke Tom grimly, "he will find that he has carried the joke too far," and with that he and the miner left the Foger home.

"It's all my fault," bewailed Abe, as he and our hero trudged on toward the Swift household.

"No, it wasn't, Abe," declared Tom. "Any one would have been deceived by such tactics as Andy used--that is any stranger. And you didn't expect to find two airship sheds so close together."

"No. That's right, I didn't. That's what threw me off th' track."

"Andy only recently began work on his triplane. I don't know what his object is, and I don't care. Just now I'm more concerned about getting back this map."

"I hope we do get it."

"Oh, we will. I'm going to start off on my own hook, to find Andy. But first I'll take you to my house."

The old miner was soon telling his story to Mr. Swift, the housekeeper and Garret Jackson. They expressed their surprise at Andy's daring act. But Tom didn't do much more talking.

"I'm going out to find Andy," he declared, "and when I do--" He didn't finish his sentence, but they all knew what he meant.

But the bully was in none of his usual haunts, though Tom visited them all. Nor was Andy at the homes of either of his cronies.

"Well, if I don't find him, I shall certainly swear out the warrant," decided Tom. "I'll give him until night, and then I'll call on the police."

Still he did not give up, but went to several other places where Andy might be found. He had about given up, as it was getting toward late afternoon, when, as he came out of a billiardroom, where the bully was in the habit of spending much of his time, Tom saw the lad of whom he was in search.

"Hold on there, Andy Foger!" cried the young inventor. "I want to see you!"

"What about?"

"You know very well. Where's that map you stole?"

"I haven't got it."

"Take care!" and Tom, with a quick step was beside the bully, and had grasped him firmly by the arm.

"You let me alone, Tom Swift!" cried Andy.

"Where's that map?" and Tom gave Andy's arm a wrench.

"It's at your house; that's where it is! I just took it back. It was only a joke."

"A joke, eh? And you took it back?"

"Yes, I did. Now you let me go!"

"I will when I find out if you're telling me the truth or not, Andy Foger. You come with me!"

"Where?"

"To my house. I want to see if that map's there."

"Well, you'll find that it is, and you'd better let me go! My father told me to take the map back, and I did. You let me go!"

Andy struggled to get loose, but Tom had too tight a grip. There was something, too, in the manner of our hero that warned Andy not to trifle with him. So, concluding that discretion was the better part of valor, Andy walked sullenly along toward Tom's home, the young inventor never relaxing the grip on his enemy's arm.

They reached the Swift home. Still holding his captive, Tom rang the bell. His father came to the door, followed by Abe Abercrombie.

"Is the map back?" asked the young inventor, anxiously.

"Yes, Andy brought it here a few minutes ago," announced Mr. Swift.

"Is it the right one, Abe?" inquired Tom.

"Yep, Tom. I made sure of that as soon as I laid my eyes on it. It's th' right one."

"Then you can go, Andy Foger," announced our hero, "and if I ever catch you in another trick like this, I'll take the law into my own hands. Clear out, now!"

"You wait! I'll get even with you," muttered the bully, as he fled down the front walk, as though afraid Tom would, even then, put his threat into execution.

"Did he damage the map any?" asked the lad, as he followed his father and Abe into the house.

"Nary a bit," answered the old miner. "It's jest th' same as it was. There it is," and he spread a crinkled sheet of tough parchment in front of Tom. It was covered with a rude drawing, and with names of places scrawled on it.

"So that's the map, eh?" murmured Tom, eagerly scanning it.

"That's it, an' here's th' valley of gold," went on Abe, as he placed one rough finger on a certain spot. "Right there--hello!" he cried, as he peered more closely at the parchment. "That ink spot wasn't there when I had th' map, a few hours ago."

"What ink spot?" asked Tom, anxiously.

"That one," and the miner indicated a small one near the edge of the map. "That was never there!"

"It looks as if it was recently made," added Mr. Swift, who was something of a chemist.

"An ink spot-freshly made," murmured Tom, "Dad--Abe, I can guess what's happened!"

"What?" demanded the miner.

"Andy Foger made a copy of this map while it was in his possession, and now he knows where the valley of gold is as well as we do! He may get there ahead of us!"

CHAPTER V
GRAVE SUSPICIONS

Tom's announcement took them all by surprise. For a moment no one knew what to say, while the young inventor looked more closely at the parchment map.

"Do you really think he has dared to make a copy of it?" asked Mr. Swift.

"I do," answered his son. "That ink spot wasn't there when Abe gave him the map; was it?"

"No," replied the miner.

"And it couldn't get on in Andy's pocket," went on Tom. "So he must have had it open near where there was ink."

"His fountain pen might have leaked," suggested Mr. Jackson.

"In that case the ink spot would be on the outside of the map, and not on the inside," declared Tom, with the instinct of a detective. "Unless he had the map folded in his pocket with the inside surface on the outside, the ink couldn't have gotten on. Besides, Andy always carries his fountain pen in his upper vest pocket, and that pocket is too small to hold the map. No, I'm almost positive that Andy or his father have sneakingly made a copy of this map!"

"I'm sorry to have to admit that Mr. Foger is capable of such an act," spoke Mr. Swift, "but I believe it is true."

"And here is another thing," went on the young inventor, who was now closely scanning the parchment through a powerful magnifying glass, "do you see those tiny holes here and there, Mr. Jackson?" "Yes," answered the engineer.

"Were they there before, Abe?" went on Tom, calling the old miner's attention to them.

"Nary a one," was the answer. "It looks as if some one had been sticking pins in th' map."

"Not pins," said Tom, "but the sharp points of a pair of dividers, or compasses, for measuring distances. Andy, or whoever made a copy of the map, used the dividers to take off distances with. This clinches it, in my mind."

"But what can you do?" asked Tom's father.

"I don't know," answered the young inventor. "It would be of little use to go to Andy. Naturally he would deny having made a copy of the map, and his father would, also. Even though I am sure they have a copy, I don't see how I am going to make them give it up. It's a hard case. There's only one thing I see to do."

"What's that?" asked Abe.

"Start for Alaska as soon as possible, and be first on hand at the valley of gold."

"Good!" cried the miner. "That's the way to talk! We'll start off at once. I know my way around that country pretty well, an' even though winter is coming on, I think we can travel in th' airship. That's one reason why I wanted t' go in one of these flyin' machines. Winter is no time to be in Alaska, but if we have an airship we won't mind it, an' it's the best time t' keep other people away, for th' ordinary miner or prospector can't do anythin' in Alaska in winter--that is away up north where we're goin'."

"Exactly where are we going?" asked Tom. "I have been so excited about discovering Andy's trick that I haven't had much time to consider where we're bound for nor what will be the best plan to follow."

"Well, we're goin' to a region about seven hundred an' fifty miles northwest from Sitka," explained the old miner, as he pointed out the location on the map. "We'll head for what they call th' Snow Mountains, an' th' valley of gold is in their midst. It's just over th' Arctic circle, an' pretty cold, let me tell you!"

"You'll be warm enough in Tom's airship, with the electric stoves going," commented Mr. Jackson.

"Well, we'll need t' be," went on the miner. "Th' valley is full of caves of ice, an' it's dangerous for th' ordinary traveler. In fact an airship was the only way I saw out of th' difficulty when I was there."

"Then you have been to the valley of gold?" asked Tom.

"Well, not exactly TO it," was the reply, "but I was where I could see it. That was in th' summer, though of course the summer there isn't like here. I'll tell you how it was."

The miner settled himself more comfortably in his chair, and resumed his story.

"It was two year ago," he said, "that me an' Jim Mace started to prospect in Alaska. We didn't have much luck, an' we kept on workin' our way farther north until we come to these Snow Mountains. Then our supplies gave out, an' if it hadn't been for some friendly Eskimos I don't know what we would have done. Jim and me we gave 'em some trinkets an' sich, and th' Indians began talkin' of a wonderful valley of gold, where th' stuff lay around in chunks on top of the ground."

"Me and Jim pricked up our ears at that, so to speak, an' we wanted to see th' place. After some delay we was taken to th' top of a big crag, some distance away from where we had been stopping with the friendly Eskimos, or Indians, as I call 'em. There, away down below, was a valley--an' a curious sort of a valley it were. It seemed filled with big bubbles--bubbles made of solid banks of snow or ice, an' we was told, me an' Jim was, that these were caves of ice, an' that th' gold was near these caves."

"Well, of course me an' my partner wanted to go down the worst way, an' try for some gold, but th' Indians wouldn't let us. They said it was dangerous, for th' ice caves were constantly fallin' in, an' smashin' whoever was inside. But to prove what they said about th' gold, they sent one of their number down, while we waited on th' side of th' mountain."

"Did he get any gold?" asked Tom, eagerly.

For answer the old miner pulled from his pocket a few yellow pebbles--little stones of dull, gleaming yellow. "There's some of th' gold from amid th' caves of ice," he remarked simply. "I kept 'em for a souvenir, hopin' some day I might git back there. Well, Jim an' me watched th' Indian going down into th' valley. He come back in about three hours, havin' only gone to th' nearest cave, an' he had two pockets filled with these little chunks of solid gold. They gave me an' Jim some, but they wouldn't hear of us goin' t' th' valley by ourselves."

"Then a bad storm come up, an' we had t' hit th' trail for home--the Indians' home, I mean--for Jim an' I was far enough away from ours."

"Well, t' make a long story short, Jim an' me tried every way we knowed t' git t' that valley, but we couldn't. It come off colder an' colder, an' th' tribe of Indians with whom we lived was attacked by some of their enemies, an' driven away from their campin' grounds. Jim an' me, we went too, but not before Jim had drawed this map on a piece of dog-skin we found in one of the huts. We had an idea we might get back, some day, an' find the valley, so we'd need a map t' go by. But poor Jim never got back. He got badly frozen when the Indians drove us an' our friends away, an' he never got over it. He died up there in th' ice, an' we buried him. I took th' map, an' when spring come, I made a hike out of that country. From then until now I've been plannin' how t' git t' that valley, an' th' only way I seen was an airship. Then, when I was prospectin' around out in Colorado I saw Tom's machine hidden in th' trees, an' I waited until he come along, which part you know as well as I do," finished Abe.

"And that's the story of the valley of gold," spoke Mr. Swift.

"That's all there is to it," assented Abe, simply.

"Do you think there is much gold there?" asked Tom.

"Plenty of it--for th' pickin' up," replied the miner. "Around th' caves of ice it's full of it, but, of course, it's dangerous. An' th' only way t' git t' it, an' pass th' savage Indians that are all around in th' mountains about th' valley, is t' fly over their heads in th' airship."

"Then that's what we'll do," decided Tom.

"Will you go all the way in the RED CLOUD?" inquired Mr. Jackson.

"No, I think I'll send the airship on ahead to some point in Washington--say Seattle," replied Tom, "put it together there, and start for the Snow Mountains. In Seattle we can get plenty of supplies and stores. It will be a good point to start from, and will save us a long, and perhaps dangerous, flight across the United States."

"I think that will be the best plan," agreed Mr. Swift. "But what about Andy--do you think he'll try to follow--or try to get ahead of you now that he has a copy of the map?"

"He may," answered Tom. "But I have a little trick I'm going to work on Andy. I will try to learn whether he really has a copy of the map, though I'm practically certain of it. Then I'll decide what's best to do."

"In th' meanwhile, will you be gettin' ready?" asked Abe. "I'd like t' start as soon as we can, for it's awful cold there, the longer you wait, at this time of th' year."

"Yes, I'll start right to work, getting the RED CLOUD in readiness to be shipped," promised Tom.

CHAPTER VI
ANDY'S AIRSHIP FLIES

H ello, Tom, have you heard the news?" asked Ned Newton, of the young inventor, a few days later.

"What news, Ned? I declare I've been so busy thinking out the best plan to ship the RED CLOUD to Seattle that I haven't been over to town. What's going on? Have they decided to build a new church in Shopton, or something like that?"

"Oh, this about Andy Foger's airship."

"Andy's airship, eh? Is he still working on it?"

"It's all done, so Sam Snedecker was telling me last night, and to-day Andy is going to try to fly it."

"You don't mean it!"

"Sure thing. Let's go over and watch him."

"He might make a fuss, same as he did when we looked in the window of his shed."

"He can't make any fuss now. He's got to take his machine out to fly it, and anybody that wants to can look on. Didn't he watch you make flights often enough?"

"That's so. Where is the trial flight going to take place?"

"In the big meadow. Come on over."

"Guess I will. I can't do much more now. I've been getting some boxes and crates made in which to pack the RED CLOUD. I'll have to take her all apart."

"Then you're really going to hunt for the valley of gold?"

"Sure thing. How about you going, Ned? I spoke to dad about it, and he said he'd see that you could have a leave of absence."

"Yes, that part's all right. The bank president told me today I could take a vacation any time I wanted it. In fact that's what I came over to see you about. I want to thank your father."

"Then you're going?"

"I sure am, Tom! Won't it be great! I hope I can get a little gold for myself! My folks didn't take very much to the notion of me going off in an airship, but I told them how often you'd gone on trips, and come safely back, so they finally gave their consent. When are you going to start?"

"Oh, in about two weeks. Did I tell you about Andy and the map?"

"No. What trick has he been up to now?"

Thereupon Tom related his suspicions concerning the bully, and also hinted to Ned of a certain ruse he intended to work on Andy when he got the chance.

"Well, if you're ready, suppose we go over and see if Andy's airship will really fly," suggested Ned, after a while. "I'm doubtful myself, and I'd just like to see him come to grief, after the many mean things he's done to you."

"Well," spoke Tom slowly, "I don't know as I wish him any bad luck, but I certainly hope he doesn't use his airship to try to beat us out in the hunt for the valley of gold."

"Do you think he might?"

"It's possible. But never mind about that now. Come on, we'll go over to the big meadow."

The two chums walked along together, talking of many things. Tom told of some communication he had had with Mr. Damon, in which letters the eccentric man had inquired as to when the trip for Alaska would be undertaken.

"Then he's going?" asked Ned.

"Oh, yes, it wouldn't seem natural to go without some of Mr. Damon's blessings. But I think he's going to bring a friend with him."

"Who?"

"Mr. Ralph Parker."

"That gloomy scientist, who is always predicting such terrible things going to happen?"

"That's the gentleman. You met him once, I believe Mr. Damon says Mr. Parker wants to do some scientific studying in the far north, so I've already counted on him as one of our party. Well, perhaps he won't do so much predicting this trip."

A little later Tom and Ned came to a big open field. They saw quite a crowd gathered in it, but no sign of an airship.

"Guess Andy hasn't arrived," spoke Tom.

"No; very likely he's found out that something is wrong with his machine, and he isn't going to risk it."

But almost as Ned spoke, there sounded cries of excitement from the crowd, and, a little later, something big and white, with many wing-shaped stretches of canvas sticking out from all sides, was seen turning into the big meadow from the broad highway that led to Andy's house.

"There she is!" cried Ned.

"There's something, at any rate," conceded Tom, as he hastened his steps. "It's a queer-looking aeroplane, though. My! he's got enough wings to it!"

"Yes, it's Andy's sure enough," went on Ned "There he is in front, giving orders like a major-general, and Sam and Pete are helping him. Let's get closer."

They followed the crowd, which was thronging about the airship that Andy Foger had made, Tom had a glimpse of the machine. It was a form of triplane, with three tiers of main wings, and several other sets of planes, some stationary and some capable of being moved. There was no gas-bag feature, but amidships was a small, enclosed cabin, which evidently held the machinery, and was designed to afford living quarters. In some respects the airship was not unlike Tom's, and the young inventor could see that Andy had copied some of his ideas. But Tom cared little about this.

"Do you think it will go up?" asked Ned.

"It looks to me to be too heavy, and his propellers seem too small," answered Tom. "He's got to have a very powerful motor to make all that bulk fly."

The people were crowding in closer around the airship, for the news that Andy was to attempt a flight had spread about town.

"Now keep back--all of you!" ordered the bully, with a show of anger. "If any one damages my airship I'll have him arrested! Keep back, now, or I won't fly!"

"Reminds me of a little kid saying he won't play if he can't have his own way," whispered Ned to Tom.

"Hello, Andy, give us a ride!"

"Going above the clouds?"

"When are you coming back?"

"Bring down a snowstorm!"

"Be careful that you don't fall!"

These were some of the things shouted at Andy, for he had few friends among the town lads, on account of his mean ways.

"Keep quiet--all of you!" he ordered. "Get back. You might get hurt when I start the motor. I'm going to make a flight soon," he added proudly. "Sam, you come over here and hold this end. Pete, you go back to the rear. Simpson, you get inside and help me with the motor. Henderson, you get ready to shove when I tell you."

These last orders were to the two machinists whom Andy had engaged to help him, and the bully gave himself no end of airs and importance as he bustled about.

Tom could not help but admit that Andy's machine was a big affair. There was a great stretch of wings and planes, several rudders other appliances for which the young inventor could not exactly fathom a use. He did not think the machine would fly far, if at all. But Andy was hurrying here and there, getting the triplane in place on a level stretch of ground, as if he intended to capture some great prize.

"Are you going to tackle him about stealing a copy of that map?" asked Ned.

"I will if I get a chance," answered Tom, in a low voice.

He got his opportunity a few minutes later. Andy, hurrying here and there, came face to face with the young inventor.

"Hello, Andy," spoke Tom, good-naturedly. "So you're going to make a flight, eh?"

"Yes, I am, and I s'pose you came around to see if you could get any ideas; didn't you?" sneered Andy.

"Of course," admitted Tom, with an easy laugh. "My airship doesn't fly, you know, Andy, and I want to see what's wrong with it."

There was a laugh in the crowd, at this, for Tom's success was well known.

"Are you going to Alaska?" suddenly asked Tom, in a low voice, of the bully.

"To Alaska? I--I don't--I don't know what you mean?" stammered Andy, as he turned aside.

"Yes, you do know what I mean," insisted Tom. "And I want to tell you that the map you have won't be of much use to you. Why, do you think," he went on, "that Abe would carry the real map around with him that way? It's easy to make a copy look like an original, Andy, and also very easy to put false distances and directions on a map that may fall into the hands of an enemy."

The shot told. Andy's face turned first red and then pale.

"A--a false map!" he stammered. "Wrong directions?"

"Yes--on the copy you made of the map you took from Mr. Abercrombie," went on Tom.

"I--I didn't make any--Oh, I'm not going to talk to you!" blustered Andy. "Get out of my way! I'm going to fly my airship."

The bully pushed past Tom, and started toward the triplane. But Tom had found out what he wanted to know. Andy had made a copy of the map. From now on there would be every danger that the bully would make an effort to get to the valley of gold.

But other matters held Andy's attention now. He wanted to try his airship. With the help of his two cronies, and the machinists, the machine was gone over, oiled up, and finally, after several false starts, the motor was set going.

It made a terrific racket, and the whole machine vibrated as though it would shake apart.

"He hasn't got if well enough braced," said Tom to Ned.

"Out of the way, now, everybody!" yelled Andy. "Keep away or you'll get hurt! I'm going up!"

He climbed into the cabin of the craft, and took his position at the steering-wheel. The speed of the motor, its racket and its stream of sparks increased.

"Let go!" cried Andy to those who were holding his craft.

They released their hold. The triplane moved slowly across the ground, gathered speed, and, then, under the impulse of the powerful propellers, ran rapidly over the meadow.

"Hurrah! There he goes!" cried Sam.

"Yes! Now he's going to fly," proudly added Pete Bailey, the other crony of the bully.

"He'd better fly soon, then, or he'll be in the ditch," said Tom grimly, for a little, sluggish stream crossed the meadow not far from where Andy had started.

The next instant, thinking he had momentum enough, Andy tilted his elevation plane. The clumsy triplane rose into the air and shot forward.

"There he goes!" cried Sam.

"Hurrah!" yelled the crowd.

Andy had gone up about ten feet, and was making slow progress.

"I guess Tom Swift isn't the only one in Shopton who can build an airship!" sneered Pete Bailey.

"Look! Look!" yelled Ned. "He's coming down!"

Sure enough, Andy's machine had reached the end of her flight. The motor stopped with something between a cough and a wheeze. Down fluttered the aeroplane, like some clumsy bird, down into the ditch, settling on one side, and then coming to rest, tilted over at a sharp angle. Andy was pitched out, but landed on the soft mud, for there had been a thaw. He wasn't hurt much, evidently, for he soon scrambled to his feet as the crowd surged toward him.

"Well, he flew a little way," observed Ned, grimly.

"But he came down mighty soon," added Tom. "I thought he would. His machine is too big and clumsy. I've seen enough. Come on, Ned. We'll get ready to go to Alaska. Andy Foger will never follow us in that machine."

But Tom was soon to find out how much mistaken he was.

CHAPTER VII
READY FOR THE TRIP

Andy Foger stood looking at his tilted airship. His clothes were covered with mud from the ditch, some of the muck had splashed over his face so that he was a pitiable looking object.

"What's the matter?" panted Pete Bailey.

"Are you hurt?" asked Sam Snedecker.

The two cronies had hurried to the side of the bully.

"Matter? Can't you see what's the matter?" demanded Andy wrathfully. "The machine came down, that's what's the matter! Why didn't you fellows fix the motor better?" he shouted at the two machinists as they came running up, followed by the crowd.

"Fix it better? The motor was all right," declared the taller machinist. "Any of them are likely to stop unexpectedly."

"Well, I didn't think mine would," came from Andy. "Now look at my airship! It's all busted!"

"No, it isn't hurt much," said the other man, after critically looking it over. "We can fix it, and you'll fly yet, Andy."

"I hope I do, if only to fool Tom Swift," declared the bully, as he wiped some of the mud from his face. "Come on, now, help me wheel the machine back, and I'll try it again."

Andy made another attempt, but this time the machine did not even rise off the ground, and then, amid the jeers of the crowd, the discomfited lad took his aeroplane back to the shed in the rear of his house.

"I'll fix it yet, and make a long flight," he declared. "I'll show Tom Swift he can't laugh at me!"

"You'll make a long flight eh?" asked one of the machinists. "Where will you go?"

"Never mind," answered Andy, with a knowing wink. "I've got a plan up my sleeve--my father and I are going to do something that will astonish everybody in Shopton," and then Andy, with many nods and winks, went into the shed, where he began giving orders about the airship. He wanted the motor changed, and one of the machinists made some suggestions about the planes, which, he said, would give better results.

As for Tom and Ned, they strolled away, satisfied that in Andy Foger they would not have a very dangerous rival, as far as airships were concerned.

Tom thought matters over during the next few days. He was now satisfied that Andy had a copy of the map, and, as far as he could see, there was no way of getting it from him, for he could not prove to the satisfaction of the legal authorities that the bully actually had it.

"We'll just have to take a chance, that's all," decided the young inventor in talking matters over with his father, Ned, and Abe Abercrombie. "If Andy and some of his crowd trail after us, we'll just have to run away from them and get to the valley first."

"If they do get there, they won't find it very easy traveling I reckon," remarked Abe. "They'll get all they want of the caves of ice. But hadn't we better get a hustle on ourselves, Tom?"

"Yes, we will soon start now. I have the RED CLOUD all packed up for shipment to Seattle. We will send it on ahead, and then follow, for it will take some time to get there, even though it's going by fast freight."

"What about Mr. Damon?" asked Ned. "When is he coming?"

"There's no telling," responded Tom. "He may be on hand any minute, and, again, he may only show up just as we are starting. I haven't heard from him in the last day or two."

At that moment there was a knock on the private office in the aeroplane shed, where Tom, Ned and Abe Abercrombie were talking.

"Who's there?" asked Tom.

"It's me," answered a voice recognizable as that of the colored man Eradicate.

"What is it, Rad?" asked Tom.

"Why I jest thought I'd tell you dat de blessin' man am comin' down de road."

"The blessing man?" repeated Tom. "Oh, you mean Mr. Damon."

"Yais, sah, dat's jest who I done mean. An' dere's anodder gen'man wif him."

"Mr. Parker, I expect," spoke Tom. "Well, tell them to come in here, Rad."

"Yais, sah. Dey's comin' up de path now, so dey is."

The next moment Tom and the others heard a voice saying:

"Why, bless my necktie! The RED CLOUD is gone!" Mr. Damon had peered into the shed, and had not seen the airship, for Tom had it packed up. "I wonder if Tom Swift has gone away? Bless my top-knot, Mr. Parker, I hope We're not too late!"

"Indeed I hope not," added the scientist. "I wish to make a study of the caves of ice. I think perhaps they may be working south, and, in time, this part of the country may be covered deep under a frozen blanket."

"Cheerful, isn't he, Ned?" asked Tom, with a smile. Then, going to the door of the shed he called out: "Here we are, Mr. Damon. Glad to see you, Mr. Parker." This last wasn't exactly true, but Tom wanted to be polite.

"Bless my collar button, Tom! But what has become of the airship?" asked Mr. Damon, as he looked about the shed, and saw only a number of boxes and crates.

"Taken apart, and packed up, ready for the trip to the valley of gold and the caves of ice," replied the young inventor, and then he briefly told of their plans.

"Well, that's a good idea," declared the eccentric man. "Mr. Parker and I are ready to go whenever you are, Tom."

"Then we'll start very soon. I will get all our supplies in Seattle. Now, to discuss details," and, after Mr. Parker and Mr. Damon had been made acquainted with the old miner, who told his story in brief, they began a discussion of the prospective trip.

Mr. Damon and Mr. Parker took up their residence in Tom's house, and while the eccentric man busied himself in helping our hero, Ned and Abe Abercrombie in getting ready for the trip to Alaska, the gloomy scientist went about making "observations" as he called them, with a view to predicting what might happen in the near future.

He was particularly anxious to get up north, among the caves of ice, and, several times he repeated his statement that he believed the mass of ice in Alaska was working down toward the south. But no one paid much attention to him, though Tom recalled, not without a little shudder, that Mr. Parker had correctly predicted the destruction of Earthquake Island, and also the landslide on Phantom Mountain.

The airship was finally sent off, being forwarded to Seattle in sections, where it could easily be put together. The matter of Andy Foger having a duplicate map of the valley of gold was discussed, but it was agreed that nothing could be done about it. So Tom and the others devoted all their energies to getting in shape for their prospective journey.

Mr. Swift was invited to go, but declined on the ground that he had several inventions to perfect, nor could Mr. Jackson go, as he was needed to help his employer. So Tom, Ned, Mr. Damon, Mr. Parker and Abe Abercrombie made up the party. Tom arranged to send wireless messages to his father from the airship once they were started off toward the valley of gold, and over the frozen north.

One evening, when Tom had been to pay a last visit to Mary Nestor, as he was coming past the Foger premises he saw a number of large vans, loaded with big packing cases coming out of the banker's yard.

"Hum! I wonder if they're moving?" mused our hero. "If they are they're taking a queer time for it." He paused a moment to look at the procession of vans. As he did so he heard the voice of Andy Foger.

"Now, I want you men to be careful of everything!" the bully called out arrogantly. "If you break anything I'll sue you for damages!"

"Oh, that cub makes me sick!" exclaimed one of the drivers as he came opposite Tom.

"What are you moving--eggs, that you have to be so careful?" asked the young inventor, in a low voice.

"Eggs? No! But it might just as well be," was the growling answer. "He's shipping an airship, all taken to pieces, and he has nervous prostration for fear it will be broken. I don't believe the old thing's any good, anyhow."

"An airship--Andy Foger sending away his airship?" gasped Tom. "Where to?"

"Some place in Alaska," was the startling reply. "Pitka or Sitka, or some such place like that. It's all in these boxes, G'lang there!" this to his horses.

"Andy sending his airship to Alaska!" murmured Tom in dismay. "Then he surely is going to make a try for that valley of gold!"

He turned away, while the snarling voice of the bully rang out on the night, urging the drivers to be very careful of the boxes and crates on their trucks.

CHAPTER VIII
A THIEF IN THE NIGHT

Tom Swift hardly knew what to think. He had scarcely believed, in spite of the fact that he was sure Andy had a copy of the map, that the bully would actually make an effort to go to the valley of gold.

"And in that airship of his, too," mused Tom. "Well, there's one consolation, I don't believe he'll go far in that, though it does sail better than when he made his first attempt. Well, if he's going to try to beat us, it's a good thing I know it We can be prepared for him, now."

Tom, after watching the big vans for a few minutes, turned and kept on toward his home.

There was more than surprise on the part of Mr. Damon and the others when Tom told his news. There was alarm, for there was a feeling that Mr. Foger and his son might adopt unscrupulous tricks.

"But what can we do?" asked Mr. Swift

"Whitewash him!" exclaimed Eradicate Sampson, who had overheard part of the conversation. "Dat's what I'd do t' him an' his father, too! Dat's what I would! Fust I'd let mah mule Boomerang kick him a bit, an' den, when he was all mussed up, I'd whitewash him!" That was the colored man's favorite method of dealing with enemies, but, of course, he could not always carry it out.

However, after considering the matter from all sides, it was decided that nothing could be done for the present.

"Let them go," said Tom, "I don't believe they'll ever find the valley of gold. I fancy I threw a scare into Andy, talking as I did about the map."

"Well, even if the Fogers do get the gold," said Mr. Parker calmly, "they cannot take away the caves of ice, and it is in them that I am most interested. I want to prove some of my new theories."

"And we need the gold," said Tom, in a low voice; "don't we, Abe?"

"That's what we do, Tom," answered the old miner.

Preparations were now practically completed for their trip to Seattle by rail. Tom made some inquiries in the next few days regarding the Fogers, but only learned that the father and son had left town, after superintending the shipment of their airship.

"Well, we start to-day," remarked Tom, as he arose one morning. "In two weeks, at most, we ought to be hovering over the valley, Abe."

"I hope so? Tom. You've got the map put away safely, have you?"

"Sure thing. Are you all ready?"

"Yes."

"Then we'll start for the depot right after breakfast." The adventurers had arranged to take a local train from Shopton, and get on a fast express at one of the more important! stations.

Good-byes were said, Mr. Swift, Mr. Jackson, Mrs. Baggert and Eradicate waving their adieus from the porch as Tom and the others started for the depot. Miss Mary Nestor had bidden our hero farewell the previous night--it being a sort of second good-bye, for Tom was a frequent caller at her house, and, if the truth must be told he rather disliked to leave the young lady.

Tom found a few of his friends at the station, who had gathered there to give him and Ned BON-VOYAGE.

"Bring us back some nuggets, Tom," pleaded Arthur Norton.

"Bring me a musk-ox if you can shoot one," suggested one.

"A live bear or a trained Eskimo for mine," exclaimed another.

Tom laughingly promised to do the best he could.

"I'll send you some gold nuggets by wireless," said Ned Newton.

It was almost time for the train to arrive. In the crowd on the platform Tom noticed Pete Bailey.

"He must feel lost without Andy," observed the young inventor to Ned.

"Yes, I wonder what he's hanging around here for?"

They learned a moment later, for they saw Pete going into the telegraph office.

"Must be something important for him to wire about," observed Ned.

Tom did not answer. The window of the office was slightly open, though the day was cool, and he was listening to the clicks of the telegraph instrument, as the operator sent Pete's message. Tom was familiar with the Morse code. What was his surprise to hear the message being sent to Andy Foger at a certain hotel in Chicago. And the message read:

"Tom Swift's party leaving to-day."

"What in the world does that mean?" thought Tom, but he did not tell Ned what he had picked up as it went over the wire. "Why should Andy want to be informed when we leave? That's why Pete was hanging around here! He had been instructed to let Andy know when we left for Seattle. There's something queer back of all this."

Tom was still puzzling over the matter when their train roiled in and he and the others got aboard.

"Well, we're off!" cried Ned.

"Yes; we're off," admitted Tom, and, to himself he added: "No telling what will happen before we get there, though."

The trip to Chicago was without incident, and, on arrival in the Windy City, Tom was on the lookout for Andy or his father, but he did not see them. He made private inquiries at the hotel mentioned in Pete's telegram, but learned that the Fogers had gone on.

"Perhaps I'm worrying too much," thought Tom. But an event that occurred a few nights later, when they were speeding across the continent showed him that there was need of great precaution.

On leaving Chicago, Tom had noticed, among the other passengers traveling in the same coach as themselves, a man who seemed to be closely observing each member of the party of gold-hunters. He was a man with a black mustache, a mustache so black, in fact, that Tom at once concluded that it had been dyed. This, in itself, was not much, but there was a certain air about the man--a "sporty" air-- which made Tom suspicious.

"I wouldn't be surprised if that man was a gambler, Ned," he said to his chum, one afternoon, as they were speeding along. The man in question was several seats away from Tom.

"He does look like one," agreed Ned.

"I needn't advise you not to fall in with any of his invitations to play cards, I suppose," went on Tom, after a pause.

"No, indeed, it's something I don't do," answered Ned, with a laugh. "But it might be a good thing to speak to Abe Abercrombie about him. If that man's a sharper perhaps Abe knows him, or has seen him, for Abe has traveled around in the West considerable."

"We'll ask him," agreed Tom, but the miner, when his attention was called to the man, said he had never seen him before.

"He does look like a confidence man," agreed Abe, "but as long as he doesn't approach us we can't do anything, and don't need to worry."

There was little need to call the attention of either Mr. Damon or Mr. Parker to the man, for Mr. Damon was busy watching the scenery, as this trip was a new one to him, and he was continually blessing something he saw or thought of. As for Mr. Parker, he was puzzling over some new theories he had in mind, and he said little to the others.

On the night of the same day on which Tom had called special attention to the man with the black mustache, our hero went to his berth rather late. He had sent some telegrams to his father and one to Miss Nestor, and, when he turned in he saw the "gambler," as he had come to call him, going into the smoking compartment of the coach. Though Tom thought of the man as a gambler, there was no evidence, as yet, that he was one, and he had made no effort to approach any of our friends, though he had observed them closely.

How long Tom had been asleep he did not know, but he was suddenly awakened by feeling his pillow move. At first he thought it was caused by the swaying of the train, and he was about to go to sleep again, when there came a movement that he knew could not have been caused by any unevenness of the roadbed.

Then, like a flash there came to Tom's mind the thought that under his pillow, in a little leather case he had made for it, was the map, showing the location of the valley of gold.

He sat up suddenly, and made a lunge for the pillow. He felt a hand being hurriedly withdrawn. Tom made a grab for it, but the fingers slipped from his grasp.

"Here! Who are you!" cried Tom, endeavoring to peer through the darkness.

"It's all right--mistake," murmured a voice.

Tom leaned suddenly forward and parted the curtains of his berth. There was a dim light burning in the aisle of the car. By the gleam of it the young inventor caught sight of a man hurrying away, and he felt sure the fellow who had put his hand under his pillow was the man with the black mustache. He confirmed this suspicion a moment later, for the man half turned, as if to look back, and the youth saw the mustache.

"He--he was after my map!" thought Tom, with a gasp.

He sat bolt upright. What should he do? To raise an alarm now, he felt, would only bring a denial from the man if he accused him. There might also be a scene, and the man might get very indignant. Then, too, Tom and his friends did not want their object made known, as it would be in the event of Tom raising an outcry and stating what was under his pillow.

He felt for the map case, opened it and saw, in the gleam of the light, that it was safe.

"He didn't get it anyhow," murmured our hero. "I guess I won't say anything until morning, though he did come like a thief in the night to see if he could steal it."

Tom glanced to where his coat and other clothing hung in the little berth-hammock, and a hasty search showed that his money and ticket were safe.

"It was the map he was after all right," mused Tom. "I'll have a talk with Mr. Damon in the morning about what's best to do. That's why the fellow has been keeping such a close watch on us. He wanted to see who had the map."

Then another thought came to Tom.

"If it was the map he was after," he whispered to himself, "he must know what it's about Therefore the Fogers must have told him. I'll wager Andy or his father put this man up to steal the map. Andy's afraid he hasn't got a copy of the right one. This is getting more and more mysterious! We must be on our guard all the while. Well, I'll see what I'll do in the morning."

But in the morning the man with the black mustache was not aboard the train, and on inquiring of the conductor, Tom learned that the mysterious stranger had gotten off at a way station shortly after midnight.

CHAPTER IX
A VANDAL'S ACT

Bless my penknife!" exclaimed Mr. Daman, the next morning, when he had been told of Tom's experience in the night, "things are coming to a pretty pass when our enemies adopt such tactics as this! What can we do, Tom? Hadn't you better let one of us carry the map?"

"Oh, I guess not," answered the young inventor. "They have had one try at me, and found that I wasn't napping. I don't believe they'll try again. No, I'll carry the map."

Tom concealed it in an old wallet, as he thought it was less likely to attract attention there than in the new case he formerly used. Still he did not relax his vigilance, and his sleep for the next few nights was uneasy, as he awakened several times, thinking he felt a hand under his pillow.

At length Ned suggested that one of them sit up part of the night, and keep an eye on Tom's berth. This was agreed to, and they divided the hours of darkness into watches, each one taking a turn at guarding the precious map. But they might have spared themselves the trouble, for no further attempt was made to get it.

"I'd just like to know what Andy Foger's plans are?" said Tom one afternoon, as they were within a few miles of Seattle. "He certainly must have made up his mind quickly, after he saw the map, about going in search of the gold."

"Maybe his father proposed it," suggested Ned. "I heard, in our bank, that Mr. Foger has lost considerable money lately, and he may need more."

"I shouldn't wonder. Well, if they are going to Sitka, Alaska, to assemble their ship, I think they'll have trouble, for supplies are harder to get there than in Seattle. But we'll soon be on our way ourselves, if nothing happens. I hope all the parts of the RED CLOUD arrive safely."

They did, as Tom learned a few hours later, when they had taken up their quarters in a Seattle hotel, and he had made inquiries at the railroad office. In the freight depot were all the boxes and crates containing the parts of the big airship, and by comparison with a list he had made, the young inventor found that not a single part was missing.

"We'll soon have her together again," he said to his friends, "and then we'll start for Alaska."

"Where are you going to assemble the airship?" asked Mr. Damon.

"I've got to hire some sort of a big shed," explained Tom. "I heard of one I think I can get. It's out at the fair grounds, and was used some time ago when they had a balloon ascension here. It will be just what I need."

"How long before we can start for the gold valley?" asked the old miner anxiously.

"Oh, in about a week," answered the lad, "that is, if everything goes well."

Tom lost no time in getting to work. He had the different parts of his airship carted to the big shed which he hired. This building was on one edge of the fair grounds, and there was a large, level space which was admirably adapted for trying the big craft, when once more it was put together.

The gold-seekers worked hard, and to such good purpose that in three days most of the ship was together once more, and the RED CLOUD looked like herself again. Tom hired a couple of machinists to aid him in assembling the motor, and some of the gas appliances and other apparatus.

"Ha! Bless my rubber shoes!" cried Mr. Damon in delight, as he looked at the big craft "This is like old times, Tom!"

"Yes, indeed," agreed our hero.

"Are you going to give it a preliminary tryout?" asked Ned.

"Oh, yes, I think we can do that to-morrow," replied Tom. "I want to know that everything is in good working shape before I trust the ship on the trip to the frozen north. There are several problems I want to work out, too, for I think I will need a different kind of gas up where the temperature is so low."

"It certainly is cold up here," agreed Ned, for they were now much farther north than when they were in Shopton, and, besides, winter was coming on. It was not the best time of the year to journey into Alaska, but they had no choice.

To delay, especially now, might mean that their enemies would get ahead of them.

"We'll be warm in the airship, though; won't we?" asked Abe.

"Oh, yes," answered Tom. "We'll be warm, and have plenty to eat. Which reminds me that I must begin to see about our stock of provisions and other supplies, for we'll soon be on our way."

Work on the airship was hastened to such good advantage the next two days that it was in shape for a trial flight, and, one afternoon, the RED CLOUD was wheeled from the shed out into big field, the gas was generated, and the motor started.

There was a little hitch, due to the fact that some of the machine adjustments were wrong, but Tom soon had that remedied and then, with the big propellers whirling around, the airship was sent scudding across the field.

Another moment and it rose like a great eagle, and sailed through the air, while a small crowd that had daily gathered in the hope of seeing a flight, sent up a cheer.

"Does it work all right?" asked Ned anxiously, as he stood in the pilothouse beside his chum.

"As good as it did in Shopton," answered the young inventor, proudly.

"Bless my pocketbook! but that's lucky," exclaimed Mr. Damon. "Then we can soon start, eh?"

"As soon as we are stocked up," replied the lad.

Tom put the airship through a number of "stunts" to test her stability and the rudder control, much to the delight of the gathering throng. Everything was found to work well, and after ascending to a considerable height, to the no small alarm of the old miner, Tom made a quick descent, with the motor shut off. The RED CLOUD conducted herself perfectly, and there was nothing else to be desired.

She was sent down to earth and wheeled back into the shed, and not without some difficulty, for the crowd, which was now very large, wanted to get near enough to touch the wonderful craft.

"To-morrow I'll arrange about the supplies and provisions, and we'll stock her up," said Tom to his companions. "Now you folks had better go back to the hotel."

"Aren't you coming?" asked Ned.

I'm going to bunk here in the shed to-night, said the young inventor.

"What for?"

"I can't take any chances now that the RED CLOUD is in shape for flying. Some of the Foger crowd might be hanging around, and break in here to damage her."

"But the watchman will be on guard," suggested Ned, for since the hiring of the shed, the young inventor had engaged a man to remain on duty all night.

"I know," answered Tom Swift, "but I'm not going to take any chances. I'll stay here with the watchman."

Ned offered to share the vigil with his chum, and, after some objection Tom consented. The others went back to the hotel, promising to return early in the morning.

Tom slept heavily that night, much heavier than he was in the habit of doing. So did Ned, and their deep breathing as they lay in their staterooms, in the cabin of the airship, told of physical weariness, for they had worked hard to re-assemble the RED CLOUD.

The watchman was seated in a chair just inside the big door of the shed, near a small stove in which was a fire to take off the chill of the big place. The guard had slept all day, and there was no excuse for him nodding in the way that he did.

"Queer, how drowsy I feel," he murmured several times. "It's only a little after midnight, too," he added, looking at his watch, "Guess I'll walk around a bit to rouse myself."

He firmly intended to do this, but he thought he would wait just a few minutes more, and he stretched out his legs and got comfortable in the chair.

Three minutes more and the watchman was asleep--sound asleep, while a strange, sweet, sickish odor seemed to fill the atmosphere about him.

There was a noise at the door of the shed, a door in which there were several cracks. A man outside laid aside something that looked like an air pump. He applied one eye to a crack, and looked in on the sleeping watchman.

"He's off," the man murmured. "I thought he'd never get to sleep! Now to get in and dose those two lads! Then I'll have the place to myself!"

There was a clicking noise about the lock on the shed door. It was not a very secure lock at best, and, under the skilful fingers of the midnight visitor, it quickly gave way. The man entered. He gave one look at the slumbering watchman, listened to his heavy breathing, and then went softly toward the airship, which looked to be immense in the comparatively small shed--taking up nearly all the space.

The intruder peered in through the cabin windows where Ned and Tom were asleep. Once more there was in the atmosphere a sickish odor. The man again worked the instrument which was like a small air pump, taking care not to get his own face too near it. Presently he stopped and listened.

"They're doped," he murmured. He arose, and took from his mouth and nose a handkerchief saturated with some chemical that had rendered him immune to the effects of the sleep-producing that he had generated. "Sound asleep," he added. Then, taking out a long, keen knife, the vandal stole toward where the great wings of the RED CLOUD stretched out in the dim light like the pinions of a bird. There was a ripping, tearing, rending sound, as the vandal cut and slashed, but Tom, Ned and the watchman slumbered on.

CHAPTER X
TOM IS HELD UP

Tom Swift stirred uneasily in his heavy sleep. He dreamed that he was again in his berth in the railroad car, and that the thief was feeling under his pillow for the map. Only, this time, there seemed to be hands feeling about his clothing, trying to locate his inner pockets.

The lad murmured something unintelligible, but he did not awaken. The fumes prevented that. However, his movements showed that the effect of the drug was wearing off. It was intended only for temporary use, and it lasted less time than it would otherwise have done in a warmer, moister climate, for the cold, crisp air that penetrated the shed from outside dispelled the fumes.

"Guess I'd better not chance it," murmured the intruder. "He may not have it on him, and if I go through all his pockets I'll wake him up. Anyhow, I've done what they paid me for. I don't believe they'll sail in this airship."

The vandal gave one glance at the sleeping lads, and stole from the cabin of the craft. He looked at his work of ruin, and then tiptoed past the slumbering watchman. A moment later and he was outside the shed, hurrying away through the night.

Several hours after this Mr. Damon and the old miner were pounding on the door of the shed. Mr. Parker, the scientist, had remained at the hotel, for he said he wanted to work out a few calculations regarding some of his theories.

"I thought we'd find them up by this time," spoke the eccentric man, as he again knocked on the door. "Tom said he had lots to do to-day."

"Maybe they are working inside, and can't hear our knocks," suggested Abe. "Try th' door."

"Bless my heart! I never thought of that," exclaimed Mr. Damon. "I believe I will."

The door swung open as he pushed it, for it had not been locked when the intruder left. The first thing Mr. Damon saw was the watchman, still asleep in his chair.

"Bless my soul!" the old man shouted. "Look at this, Abe!"

"Something's wrong!" cried the miner, sniffing the air. "There's been crooked work here! Where are the boys?"

Mr. Damon was close to the airship. He looked in the cabin window.

"Here they are, and they're both asleep, too!" he called. "And--bless my eye-glasses! Look at the airship! The planes and wings are all cut and slashed! Something has happened! The RED CLOUD is all but ruined!"

Abe hastened to his side. He looked at the damage done, and a fierce look came over his face.

"The Fogers again!" he murmured. "We'll pay 'em back for this! But first we must see to the boys!"

They needed small attention, however. The opening of the big door had let in a flood of fresh air, and this dispelled the last of the fumes. The watchman was the first to revive. The sleep caused by the chemical, sprayed from the air-pump by the vandal, had been succeeded by a natural slumber, and this was the case with Ned and Tom. They were soon aroused, and looked with wonder, not unmixed with rage, at the work done in the night.

Every one of the principal planes of the airship, each of the rudders, and some of the auxiliary wings had been cut by a sharp knife--some in several places. The canvas hung in shreds and patches, and the trim RED CLOUD looked like some old tramp airship now. Tom could scarcely repress a groan.

"Who did it?" he gasped.

"And with us here on guard!" added Ned.

"I--I must have fallen asleep," admitted the watchman in confusion.

"You were all asleep," said Mr. Damon. "I couldn't rouse you!"

"And there was th' smell of chloroform, or something like it in th' shed," added the miner.

"But look at the airship!" groaned Tom.

"Is it ruined--can't we go to the valley of gold?" asked Ned.

Tom did not answer for a few minutes. He was walking around looking at his damaged craft. The sleepy feeling was rapidly leaving him, as well as Ned and the watchman.

"Bless my watch chain!" exclaimed Mr. Damon. "What an ugly, mean piece of work. Can you repair it, Tom?"

"I think so," was the hesitating answer. "It is not as bad as I feared at first. Luckily the gas-bag has not been touched, for, if it had, we could hardly have repaired it. I can fix the wings and the rudders. The propellers have not been damaged, nor has the motor been touched. I think they must have made another attempt to take the map off me," he went on, as he looked at several pockets that had been turned inside out.

An examination of the door showed how the lock had been forced, and the adventurers could easily guess the rest. But who the midnight vandal was they could not tell, though Tom and the others were sure it was some one hired by the Fogers.

"They wanted to delay us," said Tom. "They thought this would hold us back, but it won't--for long. We'll get right to work, and make new planes and rudders. Fortunately the framework isn't hurt any."

Once Tom got into action nothing held him back. He hardly wanted to stop for meals. New canvas was ordered, and that very afternoon some of the damaged wings had been repaired. In the meanwhile the stores and provisions that had been ordered were arriving, and, under the direction of the miner and Mr. Damon were put in the RED CLOUD. Tom and Ned, with the help of a man they hired, worked diligently to replace the damaged planes and rudders. Mr. Parker came out to the airship shed, but he was of little use as a helper, for he was continually stopping to jot down some memoranda about an observation he thought of, or else he would lay aside his tools to go outside, look at the weather, and make predictions.

But Tom and the others labored to such good advantage that in three days they had repaired most of the damage done. Luckily the vandal had cut and slashed in a hurry, and his malicious work was only half accomplished. There was no clue to his identity.

No trace was seen of the Fogers, and Tom hardly expected it, for he thought they were in Sitka by this time. Nor were any suspicious persons seen hanging around the shed. The adventurers left their rooms at the hotel, and took up their quarters in the airship that would soon be their home for many days. They wanted to be where they could watch the craft, and two guards were engaged.

"We'll start to-morrow," Tom announced gaily one evening when, after a hard day's work the last of the damaged planes had been repaired.

"Start fer th' valley of gold?" asked the miner.

"Yes. Everything is in good shape now. I want to go into town, to send some messages home, telling dad we'll soon be on our way, and I also want to get a few things."

"Shall I come?" asked Ned.

"No, I'd rather you'd stay here," spoke Tom, in a low voice. "We can't take any more chances of being delayed, and, as it's pretty well known that we'll sail to-morrow, the Foger crowd may try some more of their tricks. No, I'll go to town alone, Ned. I'll soon be back, however. You stay here."

Both Tom came nearly never coming back. As he was returning from sending the messages, and purchasing a few things he needed for the trip, he passed through a dark street. He was walking along, thinking of what the future might hold for him and his companions, after they reached the caves of ice, when, just as he got to a high board fence, surrounding some vacant lots, he heard some one whisper hoarsely:

"Here he comes!"

The young inventor was on his guard instantly. He jumped back to avoid a moving shadow, but was too late. Something struck him on the back of his head, and he felt his senses leaving him. He struggled against the feeling, and he realized, even in that exciting moment, that the thick collar of his heavy overcoat, which he had turned up because of a cold wind, had, perhaps, saved him from a broken skull.

"Hold him!" commanded another voice. "I'll go through him!"

The packages dropped from Tom's nerveless fingers. He felt himself sinking down, in spite of his fierce determination not to succumb. He felt several hands moving rapidly about his body, and then he struck blindly out at the footpads.

CHAPTER XI
OFF FOR THE FROZEN NORTH

Tom Swift felt as if he was struggling in some dream or nightmare. He felt strong hands holding him and saw evil faces leering at him.

Then gradually his brain cleared. His muscles, that had been weakened by the cowardly blow, grew strong. He felt his fist land heavily on some one's face. He heard a smothered gasp of pain.

Then came the sound of footsteps running--Tom heard the "ping" of a policeman's night-stick on the sidewalk.

"Here come the cops!" he heard one voice exclaim.

"Did you get it?" asked another.

"No, I can't find it. Cut for it now!"

They released the young inventor so suddenly that he staggered about and almost fell.

The next moment Tom was looking into the face of a big policeman, who was half supporting him.

"What's the matter?" asked the officer.

"Hold-up, I guess," mumbled the lad. "There they go!" he pointed toward two dark forms slipping along down the dimly-lighted street.

The officer drew his revolver, and fired two shots in the air, but the fleeing figures did not stop.

"How did it happen?" asked the policeman. "Did they get anything from you?"

"No--I guess not," answered Tom. He saw the packages containing his purchases lying where they had fallen. A touch told him his watch and pocketbook were safe. The precious map was in a belt about his waist, and that had not been removed. "No, they didn't get anything," he assured the officer.

"I came along too quick for 'em, I guess," spoke the bluecoat. "This is a bad neighborhood. There have been several hold-ups here of late, but I was on the job too soon for these fellows. Hello, Mike," as another officer came running up in answer to the shots and the raps of the night-stick. "Couple of strong-arm-men tackled this young fellow just now. I saw something going on as I turned the corner, and I rapped and ran up. They went down that way. I fired at 'em. You take after 'em, Mike, and I'll stay here. Don't believe you can land 'em, but try! I came up too quick to allow 'em to get anything, though."

Tom did not contradict this. He knew, however, that, had the men who attacked him wished to take his watch or money, they could have done it several times before the officer arrived.

"It was the map they were after," thought Tom, "not my watch or money. This is more of the Foger's work. We must get away from here."

The policeman inquired for more particulars from Tom, who related how the hold-up had taken place. The young inventor, however, said nothing about the map he carried, letting the officer think it was an ordinary attempt at robbery, for Tom did not want any reference in the newspapers to his search for the valley of gold.

Presently the other policeman returned, having been unable to get any trace of the daring men. The two bluecoats wanted to accompany Tom back to the airship shed, for his own safety, but he declared there was no more danger, and, after having given his name, so that the affair might be reported at headquarters, he was allowed to go on his way. His head ached from the blow, but otherwise he was unhurt.

"Those fellows have been keeping watch for me," the lad reasoned, as he walked quickly toward the airship shed. "They must have been shadowing me, and they hid there until I came back. Andy Foger and his father must be getting desperate. I think I know why, too. That little dig I gave Andy about his map is bearing fruit. He begins to think it's the wrong map, and he wants to get hold of the right one. Well, they shan't if I can help it. We'll be away from here in the morning."

There was indignation and some alarm among Tom's friends when he told his story a little later that night.

"Bless my walking-stick!" cried Mr. Damon. "You'll need a bodyguard after this."

"I'd just like t' git my hands on them fellers!" exclaimed the old miner. "I'd show 'em!" and a look at his rugged frame and his muscular arms and gnarled hands showed Tom and Ned that in the event of a fight they could count much on Abe Abercrombie.

"I am glad there will be no more delays, and that we will soon be moving northward," spoke Mr. Parker, a little later. "I am anxious to confirm my theory about the advance of the ice crust, I met a man to-day who had just returned from the north of Alaska. He said that a severe winter had already set in up there. So I am anxious to get to the ice caves."

"So am I," added Tom, but it was for a different reason.

They were all up early the next morning, for there were several things to look after before they started on the trip that might bring much of danger to the adventurers. Under Tom's direction, more gas was generated, and forced into the big bag. A last adjustment was made of the planes, wing tips and rudders, and the motor was given a try-out.

"I guess everything is all right," announced the young inventor. "We'll take her out."

The RED CLOUD was wheeled from the big shed, and placed on the open lot, where she would have room to rush across the ground to acquire momentum enough to rise in the air. Tom, whenever it was practical, always mounted this way, rather than by means of the lifting gas, as, in the event of a wind, he would have better control of the ship, while it was ascending into the upper currents of air, than when it was rising like a balloon.

"All aboard!" cried the lad, as he looked to see that the course was clear. Early as it was, there was quite a crowd on hand to witness the flight, as there had been every day of late, for the population of Seattle was curious regarding the big craft of the air.

"Let her go!" cried Ned Newton, enthusiastically.

Tom took his place in the steering-tower, or pilothouse, which was forward of the main cabin. Ned was in the engine-room, ready to give any assistance if needed. Mr. Damon, Mr. Parker and Abe Abercrombie were in the main cabin, looking out of the windows at the rapidly increasing throng.

"Here we go!" cried the young inventor, as he pulled the lever starting the motor, There was a buzz and a hum. The powerful propellers whirred around like blurs of light. Forward shot the great airship over the ground, gathering speed at every revolution of the blades.

Tom tilted the forward rudder to lift the ship. Suddenly it shot over the heads of the crowd. There was a cheer and some applause.

"Off for the frozen north!" cried Ned, waving his cap.

Tom shifted the rudder, to change the course of the airship. Mr. Damon was gazing on the crowd below.

"Tom! Tom!" he cried suddenly. "There's the man with the black mustache-- the man who tried to rob you in the sleeping-car!" He pointed downward to some one in the throng.

"He can't get us now!" exclaimed Tom, as he increased the speed of the RED CLOUD, and then, taking up a telescope, after setting the automatic steering gear, Tom pointed the glass at the person whom Mr. Damon had indicated.

CHAPTER XII
PELTED BY HAILSTONES

Y es, that's the man all right," observed the lad. "But if he came here to have another try for the map, he's too late. I hope we don't land now until we are in the valley of gold." Tom passed the telescope to Ned, who confirmed the identification.

"Perhaps he came to see if we started, and then he'll report to Andy Foger or his father by telegraph," suggested Mr. Damon.

"Perhaps," admitted Tom. "Anyhow, we're well rid of our enemies--at least for a time. They can't follow us up in the air." He turned another lever and the RED CLOUD shot forward at increased speed.

"Maybe Andy will race us," suggested Ned.

"I'm not afraid of anything his airship can do," declared Tom. "I don't believe it will even get up off the ground, though he did make a short flight before he packed up to follow us. It's a wonder he wouldn't think of something himself, instead of trying to pattern after some one else. He tried to beat me in building a speeding automobile, and now he wants to get ahead of me in an airship. Well, let him try. I'll beat him out, just as I've done before."

They were now over the outskirts of Seattle, flying along about a thousand feet high, and they could dimly make out curious crowds gazing up at them. The throng that had been around the airship shed had disappeared from view behind a little hill, and, of course, the man with the black mustache was no longer visible, but Tom felt as if his sinister eyes were still gazing upward, seeking to discern the occupants of the airship.

"We're well on our way now," observed Ned, after a while, during which interval he and Tom had inspected the machinery, and found it working satisfactorily.

"Yes, and the RED CLOUD is doing better than she ever did before," said Tom. "I think it did her good to take her apart and put her together again. It sort of freshened her up. This machine is my special pride. I hope nothing happens to her on this journey to the caves of ice."

"If my theory is borne out, we will have to be careful not to get caught in the crush of ice, as it makes its way toward the south," spoke Mr. Parker with an air as if he almost wished such a thing to happen, that he might be vindicated.

"Oh, we'll take good care that the RED CLOUD isn't nipped between two bergs," Tom declared.

But he little knew of the dire fate that was to overtake the RED CLOUD, and how close a call they were to have for their very lives.

"No matter what care you exercise, you cannot overcome the awful power of the grinding ice," declared the gloomy scientist. "I predict that we will see most wonderful and terrifying sights."

"Bless my hatband!" cried Mr. Damon, "don't say such dreadful things, Parker my dear man! Be more cheerful; can't you?"

"Science cannot be cheerful when foretelling events of a dire nature," was the response. "I would not do my duty if I did not hold to my theories."

"Well, just hold to them a little more closely," suggested Mr. Damon. "Don't tell them to us so often, and have them get on our nerves, Parker, my dear man. Bless my nail-file! be more cheerful. And that reminds me, when are we going to have dinner, Tom?"

"Whenever you want it, Mr. Damon. Are you going to act as cook again?"

"I think I will, and I'll just go to the galley now, and see about getting a meal. It will take my mind off the dreadful things Mr. Parker says."

But if the gloomy scientific man heard this little "dig" he did not respond to it. He was busy jotting down figures on a piece of paper, multiplying and dividing them to get at some result in a complicated problem he was working on, regarding the power of an iceberg in proportion to its size, to exert a lateral pressure when sliding down a grade of fifteen per cent.

Mr. Damon got an early dinner, as they had breakfasted almost at dawn that morning, in order to get a good start. The meal was much enjoyed, and to Abe Abercrombie was quite a novelty, for he had never before partaken of food so high up in the air, the barograph of the RED CLOUD showing an elevation of a little over twelve thousand feet.

"It's certainly great," the old miner observed, as he looked down toward the earth below them, stretched out like some great relief map. "It sure is wonderful an' some scrumptious! I never thought I'd be ridin' one of these critters. But they're th' only thing t' git t' this hidden valley with. We might prospect around for a year, and be driven back by the Indians and Eskimos a dozen times. But with this we can go over their heads, and get all the gold we want."

"Is there enough to give every one all he wants?" asked Tom, with a quizzical smile. "I don't know that I ever had enough."

"Me either," added Ned Newton.

"Oh, there's lots of gold there," declared the old miner. "The thing to do is to get it and we can sure do that now."

The remainder of the day passed uneventfully, though Tom cast anxious looks at the weather as night set in, and Ned, noting his chum's uneasiness, asked:

"Worrying about anything, Tom?"

"Yes, I am," was the reply. "I think we're in for a hard storm, and I don't know just how the airship will behave up in these northern regions. It's getting much colder, and the gas in the bag is condensing more than I thought it would. I will have to increase our speed to keep us moving along at this elevation."

The motor was adjusted to give more power, and, having set it so that it, as well as the rudders, would be controlled automatically, Tom rejoined his companions in the main cabin, where, as night settled down, they gathered to eat the evening meal.

Through the night the great airship plowed her way. At times Tom arose to look at some of the recording instruments. It was growing colder, and this further reduced the volume of the gas, but as the speed of the ship was sufficient to send her along, sustained by the planes and wings alone, if necessary, the young inventor did not worry much.

Morning broke gray and cheerless. A few flakes of snow fell. There was every indication of a heavy storm. They were high above a desolate and wild country now, hovering over a sparsely settled region where they could see great forests, stretches of snow-covered rocks, and towering mountain crags.

The snow, which had been lazily falling, suddenly ceased. Tom looked out in surprise. A moment later there came a sound as if some giant fingers were beating a tattoo on the roof of the main cabin.

"What's that!" cried Ned.

"Bless my umbrella! has anything happened?" demanded Mr. Damon.

"It's a hail storm!" exclaimed Tom. "We've run into a big hail storm. Look at those frozen stones! They're as big as hens' eggs!"

On a little platform in front of the steering-house could be seen falling immense hailstones. They played a tattoo on the wooden planks.

"A hail storm! Bless my overshoes!" cried Mr. Damon.

"A hail storm!" echoed Mr. Parker. "I expected we would have one. The hailstones will become even larger than this!"

"Cheerful," remarked Tom in a low voice, with an apprehensive look at Ned.

"Is there any danger?" asked his chum.

"Danger? Plenty of it," replied the young inventor. "The frozen particles may rip open the gas bag." He stopped suddenly and looked at a gage on the wall of the steering-tower--a gage that showed the gas pressure.

"One compartment of the bag has been ripped open!" cried Tom. "The vapor is escaping! The whole bag may soon be torn apart!"

The noise of the pelting hailstones increased. The roar of the storm, the bombardment of the icy globules, and the moaning of the wind struck terror to the hearts of the gold-seekers.

"What's to be done?" yelled Ned.

"We must go up, to get above the storm, or else descend and find some shelter!" answered Tom. "I'll first see if I can send the ship up above the clouds!"

He increased the speed of the motor so that the propellers would aid in taking the ship higher up, while the gas-generating machine was set in operation to pour the lifting vapor into the big bag.

CHAPTER XIII
A FRIGHTENED INDIAN

The violence of the hail storm, the clatter of the frozen pellets as they bombarded the airship, the rolling, swaying motion of the craft as Tom endeavored to send it aloft, all combined to throw the passengers of the RED CLOUD into a state of panic.

"Bless my very existence!" cried Mr. Damon, "this is almost as bad as when we were caught in the hurricane at Earthquake Island!"

"I am sure that this storm is but the forerunner of some dire calamity!" declared Mr. Parker.

"I'm afraid it's all up with us," came from Abe Abercrombie, as he looked about for some way of escape.

"Do you think you can pull us through, Tom?" asked Ned Newton, who, not having had much experience in airships had yet to learn Tom's skill in manipulating them.

The young inventor alone seemed to keep his nerve. Coolly and calmly he stood at his post of duty, shifting the wing planes from moment to moment, managing the elevation rudder, and, at the same time, keeping his eye on the registering dial of the gas-generating machine.

"It's all right," said Tom, more easily than he felt. "We are going up slowly. You might see if you can induce the gas machine to do any better, Mr. Damon. We are wasting some of the vapor because of the leak in the bag, but we can manufacture it faster than it escapes, so I guess we'll be all right."

"Mr. Parker, may I ask you to oil the main motor? You will see the places marked where the oil is to go in. Ned, you help him. Here, Abe, come over here and give me a hand. This wind makes the rudders hard to twist."

The young inventor could not have chosen a better method of relieving the fears of his friends than by giving them something to do to take their minds off their own troubles. They hurried to the tasks he had assigned to them, and, in a few minutes, there were no more doubts expressed.

Not that the RED CLOUD was out of danger, Far from it. The storm was increasing in violence, and the hailstones seemed to double in number. Then, too, being forced upward as she was, the airship's bag was pelted all the harder, for the speed of the craft, added to the velocity of the falling chunks of hail, made them strike on the surface of the ship with greater violence.

Tom was anxiously watching the barograph, to note their height. The RED CLOUD was now about two and a half miles high, and slowly mounting upward. The gas machine was working to its fullest capacity, and the fact that they did not rise more quickly told Tom, more plainly than words could have done, that there were several additional leaks in the gas-bag.

"I'll take her up another thousand feet," he announced grimly. "Then, if we're not above the storm it will be useless to go higher."

"Why?" asked Ned, who had come back to stand beside his chum.

"Because we can't possibly get above the storm without tearing the ship to pieces. I had rather descend."

"But won't that be just as bad?"

"Not necessarily. There are often storms in the upper regions which do not get down to the surface of the earth, snow and hail storms particularly. Hail, you know, is supposed to be formed by drops of rain being hurled up and down in a sort of circular, spiral motion through alternate strata of air--first freezing and then warm, which accounts for the onion-like layers seen when a hailstone is cut in half."

"That is right," broke in Mr. Parker, who was listening to the young inventor. "By going down this hail storm may change into a harmless rain storm. But, in spite of that fact, we are in a dangerous climate, where we must expect all sorts of queer happenings."

"Nice, comfortable sort of a companion to have along on a gold-hunting expedition, isn't He?" asked Tom of Ned, making a wry face as Mr. Parker moved away. "But I haven't any time to think of that. Say, this is getting fierce!"

Well might he say so. The wind had further increased in violence, and while the storm of hailstones seemed to be about the same, the missiles had nearly doubled in size.

"Better go down," advised Ned. "We may fall if you don't."

"Guess I will," assented Tom. "There's no use going higher. I doubt if I could, anyhow, with all this wind pressure, and with the gas-bag leaking. Down she is!"

As he spoke he shifted the levers, and changed the valve wheels. In an instant the RED CLOUD began to shoot toward the earth.

"What's happened? What in th' name of Bloody Gulch are we up ag'in'?" demanded the old miner, springing to his feet.

"We're going down--that's all," answered Tom, calmly, but he was far from feeling that way, and he had grave fears for the safety of himself and his companions.

Down, down, down went the RED CLOUD, in the midst of the hail storm. But if the gold-seekers had hoped to escape the pelting of the frozen globules they were mistaken. The stones still seemed to increase in size and number. The gas machine register showed a sudden lack of pressure, not due to the shutting off of the apparatus.

"Look!" cried Ned, pointing to the dial.

"Yes--more punctures," said Tom, grimly.

"What's to be done?" asked Mr. Damon, who had finished the task Tom allotted to him. "Bless my handkerchief! what's to be done?"

"Seek shelter if the storm doesn't stop when we get to the earth level," answered Tom.

"Shelter? What sort of shelter? There are no airship sheds in this desolate region."

"I may be able to send the ship under some overhanging mountain crag," answered the young inventor, "and that will keep off the hailstones."

Eagerly Tom and Ned, who stood together in the pilothouse peered forward through the storm.

The wind was less violent now that they were in the lower currents of air, but the hail had not ceased.

Suddenly Tom gave a cry. Ned looked at him anxiously. Had some new calamity befallen them? But Tom's voice sounded more in relief than in alarm. The next instant he called:

"Look ahead there, Ned, and tell me what you see."

"I see something big and black," answered the other lad, after a moment's hesitation. "Why, it's a big black hole!" he added.

"That's what I made it out to be," went on Tom, "but I wanted to be sure. It's the opening to a cave or hole in the side of the mountain. I take it."

"You're right," agreed Ned.

"Then we're safe," declared Tom.

"Safe? How?"

"I'm going to take the RED CLOUD in there out of the storm."

"Can you do it? Is the opening big enough?"

"Plenty. It's larger than my shed at home, Jove! but I'm glad I saw that in time, or there would have been nothing left of the gas-bag!"

With skilful hands Tom turned the rudders and sent the airship down on a slant toward the earth, aiming for the entrance to the cave, which loomed up in the storm. When the craft was low enough down so that the superstructure would not scrape the top of the cave, Tom sent her ahead on the level. But he need have had no fears, for the hole was large enough to have admitted a craft twice the size of the RED CLOUD.

A few minutes later the airship slid inside the great cavern, as easily as if coming to rest in the yard of Tom's house. The roof of the cave was high over their heads, and they were safe from the storm. The cessation from the deafening sound of the pelting hailstones seemed curious to them at first.

"Well, bless my shoelaces! if this isn't luck!" cried Mr. Damon, as he opened the door of the cabin, and looked about the cave in which they now found themselves. It was comparatively light, for the entrance was very large, though the rear of the cavern was in gloom.

"Yes, indeed, we got to it just in time,'" agreed Tom. "Now let's see what sort of a place it is. We'll have to explore it."

"There may be a landslide, or the roof may come down on our heads," objected Mr. Parker.

"Oh, my dear Parker! please be a little more cheerful," begged Mr. Damon.

The adventurers followed Tom from the airship, and all but the young inventor gazed curiously at the interior of the cave. His first thought was for his airship. He glanced up at the gas-bag, and noted several bad rents in it.

"I hope we can fix them," Tom thought dubiously.

But the attention of all was suddenly arrested by something that occurred just then. From the dark recess of the cavern there sounded a fearful yell or scream. It was echoed back a thousand-fold by the rocky walls of the cave, Then there dashed past the little group of gold-seekers a dark figure.

"Look out! It's a bear!" shouted Mr. Damon. "A bear! It's an Eskimo Indian!" yelled Abe Abercrombie, "an' he's skeered nigh t' death! Look at him run!"

As they gazed toward the lighted entrance of the cave they saw leaping and running from it an Indian who quickly scudded out into the hail storm.

"An Indian," exclaimed Tom. "An Indian in the cave! If there's one, there may be more. I guess we'd better look to our guns. They may attack us!" and he hurried back into the airship, followed by Ned and the others.

CHAPTER XIV
THE RIVAL AIRSHIP

Well armed, the adventurers again ventured out into the cave. But they need not have been alarmed so soon, for there were no signs of any more Indians.

"I guess that one was a stray Eskimo who took shelter in here from the storm," said Abe Abercrombie.

"Are we in the neighborhood of the Alaskan Indians and Eskimos?" inquired Ned.

"Yes, there are lots of Indians in this region," answered the old miner, "but not so many Eskimos. A few come down from th' north, but we'll see more of them, an' fewer of th' pure-blooded Indians as we get nearer th' valley of gold. Though t' my mind th' Indians an' Eskimos are pretty much alike."

"Well, if we don't have to defend ourselves from an attack of Indians, suppose we look over the airship," proposed Tom.

"It's too dark to see very much," objected Ned. But this was overcome when Tom started up a dynamo, and brought out a portable search-light which was played upon the superstructure of the RED CLOUD. The gas-bag was the only part of the craft they feared for, as the hailstones could not damage the iron or wooden structure and the planes were made in sections, and in such a manner that rents in them could easily be repaired. So, in fact, could the gas-bag be mended, but it was harder work.

"Well, she's got some bad tears in her," announced Tom as the light flashed over the big bag. "Luckily I have plenty of the material, and some cement, so I think we can mend the rents, though it will take some days. Nothing could have been better for us than this cave. We'll stay here until we're ready to go on."

"Unless the Indians drive us out," said Abe, in a low tone.

"Why, do you think there is any danger of that?" inquired Tom.

"Well, th' brown-skinned beggars aren't any too friendly," responded the old miner. "Th' one that was in here will be sure to tell th' others of some big spirit that flew into th' cave, an' they'll be crowdin' around here when th' storm's over. It may be we can fight 'em off, though."

"Maybe they won't attack us," suggested Ned, hopefully. "Perhaps we can make them believe we are spirits, and that it will be unlucky to interfere with us."

"Perhaps," admitted Abe, "though my experience has been that these Indians are a bad lot. They haven't much respect for spirits of any kind, an' they'll soon find out we're human. But then, we'll wait an' see what happens."

"And, in the meantime, have something to eat," put in Mr. Damon. "Bless my knife and fork! but the hail storm gave me an appetite."

In fact, there were few things which did not give Mr. Damon an appetite, Tom thought with a smile. But the meal idea was considered very timely, and soon the amateur cook was busy in the galley of the airship, whence speedily came savory odors. The electric lights were switched on, and the adventurers were quickly made comfortable in the cave, which so well sheltered the RED CLOUD. Tom completed his inspection of the craft, and was relieved to find that while there were a number of small rents, none was very large, and all could be mended in time.

Abe Abercrombie took a look outside the cave after the meal had been served. The old miner declared that they had made a good advance on their northern journey for, though he could not tell their exact location, he knew by the character of the landscape that they had passed the boundaries of Alaska.

"A few more days' traveling at the rate we came will bring us to the Snow Mountains and the valley of gold," he said.

"Well, we won't average such speed as we did during the hail storm," said Tom. "The wind of that carried us along at a terrific pace. But we will get there in plenty of time, I think."

"Why; is there any particular rush?" asked Ned.

"There's no telling when the Fogers may appear," answered the young inventor in a low voice. "But now we must get to work to repair damage."

The hail storm had ceased, and, with the passing of the clouds the cave was made lighter. But Tom did not depend on this, for he set up powerful searchlights, by the gleams of which he and his companions began the repairing of the torn gas-bag.

They worked all the remainder of that day, and were at it again early the next morning, making good progress.

"We can go forward again, in about two days," spoke Tom. "I want to give the cement on the patches plenty of chance to dry."

"Then I will have time to go out and make some observations, will I not?" asked Mr. Parker. "I think this cave is a very old one, and I may be able to find some evidences in it that the sea of ice is slowly working its way down from the polar regions."

"I hope you don't," whispered Ned to Tom, who shook his head dubiously as the gloomy scientist left the cave.

The weather was very cold, but, in the cavern it was hardly noticed. The adventurers were warmly dressed, and when they did get chilly from working over the airship, they had but to go into the well-heated and cozy cabin to warm themselves.

It was on the third day of their habitation in the cave, and work on putting the patches on the gas-bag was almost finished. Mr. Parker had gone out to make further observations, his previous ones not having satisfied him. Tom was on an improvised platform, putting a patch on top of the bag, when he heard a sudden yell, and some one dashed into the cavern.

"They're coming! They're coming!" cried a voice, and Tom, looking down, saw Mr. Parker, apparently in a state of great fear.

"What's coming?" demanded the young inventor, "the icebergs?"

"No--the Indians!" yelled the scientist. "A whole tribe of them is rushing this way!"

"I thought so!" cried Abe Abercrombie. "Where's my gun?" and he dashed into the airship.

Tom slid down off the platform.

"Get ready for a fight!" he gasped. "Where are you, Ned?"

"Here I am. We'd better get to the mouth of the cave, and drive 'em back from there."

"Yes. If I'd only thought, we could have blockaded it in some way. It's as big as a barn now, and they can rush us if they have a mind to. But we'll do our best!"

The adventurers were now all armed, even to Mr. Parker. The scientist had recovered from his first fright, when he spied the Indians coming over the snow, as he was "observing" some natural phenomenon. Tom, even in his excitement, noticed that the professor was curiously examining his gun, evidently more with a view to seeing how it was made, and on which principle it was operated, rather than to discover how to use it.

"If it comes to a fight, just point it at the Indians, pull the trigger, and work that lever," explained the young inventor. "It's an automatic gun."

"I see," answered Mr. Parker. "Very curious. I had no idea they worked this way."

"Oh, if I only had my electric rifle in shape!" sighed Tom, as he dashed forward at the side of Ned.

"Your electric rifle?"

"Yes, I've got a new kind of weapon--very effective. I have it almost finished. It's in the airship, but I can't use it just yet. However, maybe these repeaters will do the work."

By this time they were at the entrance of the cave, and, looking out they saw about a hundred Indians, dressed in furs, striding across the snowy plain that stretched out from the foot of the mountain in which was the cavern.

"They're certainly comin' on," observed Abe, grimly. "Git ready for 'em, boys!"

The gold-seekers lined up at the mouth of the cave, with guns in their hands. At the sight of this small, but formidable force, the Indians halted. They were armed with guns of ancient make, while some had spears, and others bows and arrows. A few had grabbed up stones as weapons.

There appeared to be a consultation going on among them, and, presently, one of the number, evidently a chief or a spokesman, gave his gun to one of his followers, and, holding his hands above his head, while he waved a rag that might have once been white, came forward.

"By Jove!" exclaimed Tom. "It's a flag of truce! He wants to talk with us I believe!"

"Bless my cartridges!" exclaimed Mr. Damon. "Can they speak English?"

"A little," answered Abe Abercrombie. "I can talk some of their lingo, too. Maybe I'd better see what they want."

"I guess it would be a good plan," suggested Tom, and, accordingly the old miner stepped forward. The Indian came on, until Abe motioned for him to halt.

"I reckon that's as far as it'll be healthy for you t' come," spoke Abe, grimly. "Now what do you fellers want?"

Thereupon there ensued a rapid exchange of jargon between the miner and the Indian. Abe seemed much relieved as the talk went on, until there came what seemed like a demand on the part of the dark-hued native.

"No, you don't! None of that!" muttered Abe. "If you had your way you'd take everything we have."

"What is it? What does he want?" asked Tom in a low voice.

"Why, the beggar began fair enough," replied the miner. "He said one of their number had been in the cave when a storm came an' saw a big spirit fly in, with men on its back. He ran away an' now others have come to see what it was. They don't guess it's an airship, for they've never seen one, but they know we're white folks, an' they always want things white folks have got."

"This fellow is a sort of chief, an' he says the white folks?--that's us, you know?--have taken th' Indians' cave. He says he doesn't want t' have any trouble, an' that we can stay here as long as we like, but that we must give him an' his followers a lot of food. Says they hain't got much. Land! Those beggars would eat us out of everything we had if we'd let 'em!"

"What are you going to tell them?" inquired Mr. Damon.

"I'm goin' t' tell 'em t' go t' grass, or words t' that effect," replied Abe. "They haven't any weapons that amount t' anything, an' we can stand 'em off. Besides, we'll soon be goin' away from here; won't we, Tom?"

"Yes, but--"

"Oh, there's no use givin' in to 'em," interrupted Abe. "If you give 'em half a loaf, they want two. Th' only way is t' be firm. I'll tell 'em we can't accommodate 'em."

Thereupon he began once more to talk to the Indians in their own tongue. His words were at first received in silence, and then angry cries came from the natives. The chief made a gesture of protest.

"Well, if you don't like it, you know what you kin do!" declared Abe. "We've got th' best part of our journey before us, an' we can't give away our supplies. Go hunt food if you want it, ye lazy beggars!"

The peaceful demeanor of the Indians now turned to rage. The leader dropped the rag that had served for a flag of truce, and took back his gun.

"Look out! There's going to be trouble!" cried Tom.

"Well, we're ready for 'em!" answered Abe, grimly.

There was a moment of hesitation among the natives. Then they seemed to hold a consultation with the chief. It was over shortly. They broke into a run, and quickly advanced toward the cave. Tom and the others held their guns in readiness.

Suddenly the Indians halted. They gazed upward, and pointed to something in the air above their heads. They gave utterance to cries of fear.

"What is it; another storm coming?" asked Tom.

"Let's look," suggested Ned. He and Tom stepped to the mouth of the cave--they went outside. There was little danger from the natives now, as their attention was fixed on something else.

A moment later Tom and Ned saw what this was.

Floating in the air, almost over the cave, was a great airship--a large craft, nearly the size of the RED CLOUD. Hardly able to believe the evidence of their eyes, Tom and Ned watched it. Whence had it come? Whither was it going?

"It's a triplane!" murmured Ned.

"A triplane!" repeated Tom. "Yes--it is--and it's the airship of Andy Foger! Our rivals are on our track!"

He continued to gaze upward as the triplane shot forward, the noise of the motor being plainly heard. Then, with howls of fear, the Indians turned and fled. The rival airship had vanquished them.

CHAPTER XV
THE RACE

Astonished and terrified as the Indians had been at the sight of the big-winged craft, high in the air above their heads, Tom and the others were no less surprised, though, of course, their fear was not exactly the same as that of the Alaskan natives.

"Do you really think that is Andy Foger?" asked Ned, as they watched the progress of the triplane.

"I'm almost sure of it," replied Tom. "That craft is built exactly as his was, but I never expected him to have such good luck sailing it."

"It isn't going very fast," objected Ned.

"No, but it can navigate pretty well, and that's something. He must have hustled to get it together and reach this point with it."

"Yes, but he didn't have to travel as far as we did," went on Ned. "He put his ship together at Sitka, and we came from Seattle."

"Bless my memoranda book!" exclaimed Mr. Damon. "The Fogers here! What's to be done about it?"

"Nothing, I guess," answered Tom. "I'd just as soon they wouldn't see us. I don't believe they will. Get back into the cave. We must use strategy now to get ahead of them. There will be a race to the valley of gold."

"Well, he served us one good turn, anyhow, though he didn't mean to," put in Abe Abercrombie.

"How?" asked Mr. Parker, who was still examining his gun, as though trying to understand it.

"He scared away them pesky natives," went on the miner. "Otherwise we might have had a fight, an' while I reckon we could have beat 'em, it's best not to fight if you kin git out of it."

The gold-seekers had withdrawn inside the mouth of the cave, where they could watch the progress of the rival airship without being seen. The Indians had disappeared beyond a snow-covered hill.

The airship of Andy Foger, for such it subsequently proved to be, floated slowly onward. Its progress was not marked with the speed of Tom's craft, though whether or not the occupants of the ANTHONY (as Andy had vain-gloriously named his craft after himself) were speeding up their motor, was a matter of conjecture.

The adventurers held a short consultation, while standing at the mouth of the cave watching the progress of the ANTHONY. It rose in the air, and circled about.

"He certainly IS trying to pick us up," declared Ned.

"Well, we'll start out after him to-morrow," decided Tom. "I think all the patches will hold then."

They resumed work on the RED CLOUD, and that night Tom announced that they would start in the morning. Meanwhile Andy's craft had disappeared from sight. There was no further evidence of the Indians.

"I don't reckon they'll come back," spoke Abe, grimly. "They think we are sure-enough spirits, now, able to call creatures out of the air whenever we want 'em. But still we must be on our guard."

As Mr. Parker was not of much service in helping on the airship he agreed to be a sort of guard and took his place just outside the cave, where he could make "observations," and, at the same time watch for the reappearance of Indians. They had little fear of an attack at night, for Abe said the Alaskans were not fond of darkness.

The cold seemed to increase, and, even in the sheltered cave the adventurers felt it. There were several heavy flurries of snow that afternoon, and winter seemed setting in with a vengeance. The daylight, too, was not of long duration, for the sun was well south now, and in the far polar regions it was perpetual night.

After a brief inspection of the ship the next morning, following a good night's rest, when they were not disturbed by any visits from the natives, Tom announced that they would set sail. The day was a clear one, but very cold, and the gold-seekers were glad of the shelter of the warm cabin.

The RED CLOUD was wheeled from the cave, and set on a level place. There was not room enough to make a flying start, and ascend by means of the planes and propellers, so the gas-bag method was used. The generating machine was put in operation, and soon the big red bag that hovered over the craft began to fill. Tom was glad to see that none of the several compartments leaked. The bag had been well repaired.

Suddenly the RED CLOUD shot up in the air. Up above the towering snow-covered crags it mounted, and then, with a whizz and a roar, the propellers were set going.

"Once more northward bound!" cried Tom, as he took his place in the pilot-house.

"And we'll see if we can beat Andy Foger there," added Ned.

All that morning the RED CLOUD shot ahead at good speed. The craft had suffered no permanent damage during her fight with the hail storm, and was as good as ever. They ate dinner high in the air, while sailing over a great stretch of whiteness, where the snow lay many feet deep on the level, and where great mountain crags were so covered with the glistening mantle and a coating of ice as to resemble the great bergs that float in the polar sea.

"I wouldn't want to be wrecked here," said Ned, with a shudder, as he looked down. "We'd never get away. Does any one live down there, Abe?"

"Yes, there are scattered tribes of Indians and Alaskan natives. They live by hunting and fishing, and travel around by means of dog sledges. But it's a dreary life. Me an' my partner had all we wanted of it. An airship for mine!"

"I wonder what's become of Andy?" spoke Tom, that afternoon. "I haven't sighted him, and I've been using the powerful telescope. I can't pick him up, though he can't be so very far ahead of us."

"Let me try," suggested Ned. "Put her up a bit, Tom, where I can look down. Andy won't dare go very high. Maybe I can sight him."

The RED CLOUD shot upward as the young inventor shifted the elevation rudder, and the bank clerk, with the powerful glass to his eye, swept the space below him. For half an hour he looked in vain. Then, with a little start of surprise he handed the glass to his chum.

"See what you make that out to be," suggested Ned. "It looks like a big bird, yet I haven't seen any other birds to-day."

Tom looked. He peered earnestly through the telescope for a minute, and then cried:

"It's Andy's airship! He's ahead of us! We must catch him! Ned, you and Mr. Damon speed up the motor! The race is on!"

In a few minutes the great airship was hurling herself through space, and, in less than ten minutes Andy's craft could be made out plainly with the naked eye. Fifteen minutes more and the RED CLOUD was almost up to her. Then those aboard the ANTHONY must have caught sight of their pursuers, for there was a sudden increase in speed on the part of the unscrupulous Foger crowd, who sought to steal a march on Tom and his friends.

"The race is on!" repeated the young inventor grimly, as he pulled the speed lever over another notch.

CHAPTER XVI
THE FALL OF THE ANTHONY

Had it not been for what was at stake, the race between the two big airships would have been an inspiring one to those aboard Tom's craft. As it was they were too anxious to overcome the unfair advantage taken by Andy to look for any of the finer points in the contest of the air.

"There's no denying that he's got a pretty good craft there," conceded Tom, as he watched the progress of his rival. "I never thought Andy Foger could have done it."

"He didn't do very much of it," declared Ned. "He hired the best part of that made. Andy hasn't any inventive ideas. He probably said he wanted an airship, and his dad put up the money and hired men to build it for him. Andy, Sam and Pete only tinkered around on it."

Later Tom and his chum learned that this was so--that Mr. Foger had engaged the services of an expert to make the airship. This man had been taken to Sitka with the Fogers, and had materially aided them in re-assembling the craft.

"Do you think he can beat us?" asked Ned, anxiously.

"No!" exclaimed Tom, confidently. "There's only one craft that can beat my RED CLOUD and that's my monoplane the BUTTERFLY. But I have in mind plans for a speedier machine than even the monoplane. However I haven't any fear that Andy can keep up to us in this craft. I haven't begun to fly yet, and I'm pretty sure, from the way his is going, that he has used his limit of speed."

"Then why don't you get ahead of him?" asked Mr. Damon. "Bless my tape-measure! the way to win a race is to beat."

"Not this kind of a race," and the young inventor spoke seriously. "If I got ahead of Andy now, he'd simply trail along and follow us. That's his game. He wants me to be the path-finder, for, since I cast a doubt on the correctness of the map, a copy of which he stole, he isn't sure where he's going. He'd ask nothing better than to follow us."

"Then what are you going to do if you don't get ahead of him?" asked Ned.

"I'm going to press him close until night," answered Tom, "and when it's dark, I'm going to shoot ahead, and, by morning we'll be so far away that he can't catch up to us."

"Good idea! That's th' stuff!" cried Abe with enthusiasm.

"He's a sneak!" burst out Mr. Damon. "I'd like to see him left behind."

Tom carried out his plan. The remainder of the day he hung just on Andy's flank, sometimes shooting high up, almost out of sight, and again coming down, just to show what the RED CLOUD could do when pressed.

As for those aboard the ANTHONY, they seemed to be trying to increase their speed, but, if that was their object they did not have much success, for the big, clumsy triplane only labored along.

"I wonder who he's got with him?" said Ned, as darkness was closing down. "I can't make out any one by this glass. They stick pretty closely to the cabin."

"Oh, probably Andy's father is there," said "and, perhaps, some of Mr. Foger's acquaintances. I guess Mr. Foger is as anxious to get this gold as Andy is."

"He certainly needs money," admitted Ned. "Jove! but I hope we beat him!"

But alas for Tom's hopes! His plan of waiting until night and then putting on such speed as would leave Andy behind could not be carried out. It was tried, but something went wrong with the main motor, and only half power could be developed. Tom and Ned labored over it nearly ail night, to no effect, and through the hours of darkness they could see the lights from the cabin of the ANTHONY gleaming just ahead of them. Evidently the bully's airship could not make enough speed to run away from the RED CLOUD, or else it was the plan of the Foger crowd to keep in Tom's vicinity.

The direction held by Andy's craft was a general northwestern one, and Tom knew, in time, and that very soon, it would bring the ANTHONY over the valley of gold. Evidently Andy was placing some faith in his copy of the stolen map.

"Once I get this motor in shape I'll soon pull away from him," announced Tom, about four o'clock that morning, while he and Ned, aided by Mr. Damon, were still laboring over the refractory machine.

"What are you going to do?" asked Ned.

"It's too late to carry out my original plan," went on Tom. "We're getting so near the place now that I want to be there ahead of every one else. So as soon as we can, I'm going to push the RED CLOUD for all she's worth, and get to the valley of gold first. If possession is nine points of the law, I want those nine points."

"That's the way to talk!" cried Abe. "Once we git on th' ground we kin hold our own!"

It was breakfast time before Tom had the motor repaired, and he decided to have a good meal before starting to speed up his craft. He felt better after some hot coffee, for he and the others were weary from their night of labor.

"Now for the test!" he cried, as he went back to the engine-room. "Here's where we give Andy the go-by, and I don't think he can catch us!"

There was an increasing hum to the powerful motor, the great propellers whirled around at twice their former number of revolutions, and the airship suddenly shot ahead.

Those on the ANTHOMY must have been watching for some such move as that, for, no sooner had Tom's craft begun to creep up on his rival than the forward craft also shot ahead.

But the airship was not built that could compete with Tom's. Like a racer overhauling a cart-horse, the RED CLOUD whizzed through the air. In a spirit of fun the young inventor sent his machine within a few feet of Andy's. He had a double purpose in this, for he wanted to show the bully that he did not fear him, and he wanted to see if he could discover who was aboard.

Tom did catch a glimpse of Andy and his father in the cabin of the ANTHONY, and he also saw a couple of men working frantically over the machinery.

"They're going to try to catch us!" called Tom to Ned.

This was evident a moment later, for, after the RED CLOUD had forged ahead, her rival made a clumsy attempt to follow. The ANTHONY did show a burst of speed, and, for a moment Tom was apprehensive lest he had underrated his rival's prowess.

Suddenly Ned, who was looking from a projecting side window of the pilot-house, back toward Andy's ship, cried out in alarm.

"What's the matter?" shouted Tom.

"The airship--Andy's--two of the main wings have collapsed!"

Tom looked. It was but too true. The strain under which the ANTHONY had been put when the machinists increased the speed, had been too much for the frame. Two wings broke, and now hung uselessly down, one on either side. The ANTHONY shot toward the snow-covered earth!

"They're falling!" cried Mr. Parker.

"Yes," added Tom, grimly, "the race is over as far as they are concerned."

"Bless my soul! Won't they be killed?" cried Mr. Damon.

"There's not much danger," replied the young inventor. "They can vol-plane back to earth. That's what they're doing," he added a moment later, as he witnessed the maneuver of the crippled craft. "They're in no danger, but I don't believe they'll get to the valley of gold this trip!"

Tom was soon to learn how easily he could be mistaken.

CHAPTER XVII
HITTING THE ICE MOUNTAIN

Onward sped the RED CLOUD. For a moment after the accident to Andy's ship, Tom had slowed up his craft, but he soon went on again, after he had satisfied himself that his enemies were in no danger.

"Don't you think--that is to say--I know they can't expect anything from us," spoke Mr. Damon, "but for humanity's sake, hadn't we better stop and help them, Tom?"

"I hardly think so," replied the young inventor. "In the first place they would hardly thank us for doing so, and, in the second, I don't believe they need help. They are almost safely down now."

"I don't just mean that," went on the odd man. "But they may starve to death. This is a very desolate country over which we are sailing."

"They must have a supply of food in their ship," declared Tom, "and they have brought their plight on themselves."

"They're in no great danger," put in Abe.

"There are plenty of natives around here, an' if the Fogers need food or aid they can git it by payin' for it. Why, for the sake of th' parts of their damaged airship, th' Eskimos would take th' whole party back t' Sitka and feed 'em well on th' trip. Oh, they're all right."

"Very well, if you say so," assented Mr. Damon. He looked back to watch the ANTHONY slowly settling to earth. It came gently down, proving that Tom knew whereof he spoke, when he had said they could vol-plane down. Before the RED CLOUD was out of sight Tom and his companions saw Andy and his father leave their wrecked craft and venture out on the snow-covered ground. The Fogers gazed enviously after the airship of our hero as they saw him still forging toward the goal.

"I guess Andy's stolen map won't be of much use to him," mused Tom. "Now we can put on all the speed we like," and with that he shifted the gears and levers until the airship was making exceedingly good time toward the valley of gold.

The remainder of that day saw our adventurers pursuing their way eagerly. At times they were flying high, and again, when Abe suggested that they go down to observe the character of the country over which they were passing, they skimmed along, just above the big mountains, which seemed almost like icebergs, so covered were they with frost and snow.

They were indeed in a wild and desolate country. Below them stretched a seemingly endless waste of snow and ice--great forests interspersed with treeless patches, while now and then they sailed over a frozen lake.

Once in a while they had glimpses of bands of Indians, dressed in furs, hunting. At such times the natives would look up, on hearing the noise made by the motor of the airship, and catching a glimpse of what must have seemed to them like some supernatural object, they would fall down prostrate in amazement and fear.

"Airships are pretty much of a novelty up here," remarked Abe with a grim smile.

The weather was new very cold, and the gold-seekers had to get out their heavy fur garments, of which they had brought along a goodly supply. True, it was warm in the cabin of the airship, but at times, they wanted to venture out on the deck to get fresh air, or to make some adjustments to the wing planes, and, on such occasions the keen, frosty air, as it was driven past them by the motion of the craft, made even the thickest garments seem none too warm. Then, too, it was colder at the elevation at which they flew than down on the ground.

Another day found them in a still wilder and more desolate part of Alaska. There were scarcely any signs of habitation now, and the snow and ice seemed so thick that even a long summer of sunshine could hardly have melted it. The hours of daylight, too, were growing less and less the farther north they went.

"Do you think you can pilot us right to the Snow Mountains, Abe?" asked Tom, on the third day after the accident to Andy's airship. "Let's get out the map, and have another look at it. We must be getting near the place now. We'll look at the map."

The young inventor went to his stateroom where he kept the important document in a small desk, and the others heard him rummaging around. He muttered impatiently, and Ned heard his chum say: "I thought sure I put it in here." Then ensued a further search, and presently Tom came out, his face wearing rather a puzzled and worried look, and he asked: "Say, Abe, I didn't give that map back to you; did I?"

"Nope," answered the miner. "I ain't seen it since just before th' hail storm. We was lookin' at it then."

"That's when I remember it," went on Tom, "and I thought I put it in my desk. I didn't, by any possible chance give it to you; did I, Ned?"

"Me? No, I haven't seen it."

"That's funny," went on Tom. "I'll look once more. Maybe it got under some papers."

They heard him rummaging again in his desk.

"Bless my bank-book!" cried Mr. Damon. "I hope nothing has happened to that map. We can't find the valley of gold without it."

Tom came back again.

"I can't find it." he said, hopelessly.

Then ensued a frantic search. Every possible place in the airship was looked into, but the precious map did not turn up.

"Perhaps the Fogers took it," suggested Mr. Parker, who had helped in the hunt, in a dreamy sort of fashion.

"That's not possible," said Tom. "They haven't been near enough to us since I saw the map last. No, the last time I had it was just before the hail storm, and, in the excitement of repairing the ship, I have mislaid it."

"Maybe it's back there in the big cave," suggested Ned.

"It's possible," admitted the young inventor. "Pshaw! It's very careless of me!"

"If you think it's in the cave, we'd better go back there and have a hunt for it," suggested Mr. Damon. "Otherwise we are on a wild-goose chase."

"Don't go back!" exclaimed old Abe. "I think we can find th' valley of gold without th' map, now that we have come this far. I sort of remember th' marks on that parchment, an' we are in the right neighborhood now, for I kin see some of th' landmarks my partner and I saw. I say, let's keep on! We can cruise around a bit until we strike th' right place. That won't take us so long as it would to go back to the cave. Besides, if we go back, the Fogers may get ahead of us!"

"With their broken airship?" asked Ned

"Can't they repair it?" demanded Abe.

"Hardly--up in this wild country," was Tom's opinion. "But perhaps it WILL be just as well to keep on. I have a hazy remembrance of the distances and directions on the map, and, though it will take longer to hunt out the valley this way, I think we can do it. I can't forgive myself for my carelessness! I should have kept a copy of the map, or given one of you folks one."

But they would not hear of him blaming himself, and said it might have happened to any one. It was decided that the map must be lost in the big cave, and if it was there it was not likely to be found by their enemies.

"We'll jest have t' prospect about a bit," declared Abe, "only we'll do it in th' air instead of on th' ground."

It was dusk when the fruitless search for the map was over, and they sat in the cabin discussing matters. The lights had not yet been switched on, and the RED CLOUD was skimming along under the influence of the automatic rudders and the propellers.

"Well, suppose we have supper," proposed Mr. Damon, who seemed to think eating a remedy for many ills, mental and bodily. "Bless my desert-spoon, but I'm hungry!"

He started toward the galley, while Tom went forward to the pilothouse. Hardly had he reached it than there came a terrific crash, and the airship seemed tossed back by some giant hand. Every one was thrown off his feet, and the lights which had been turned on suddenly went out.

"What's the matter?" cried Ned.

"Have we hit anything?" demanded Mr. Damon.

"Hit anything! I should say we had!" yelled Tom. "We've knocked a piece off a big mountain of ice!"

As he spoke the airship began slowly settling toward the earth, for her machinery had been stopped by the terrific impact.

CHAPTER XVIII
A FIGHT WITH MUSK OXEN

C an I help you, Tom? What's to be done?" demanded Ned Newton, as he rushed to where his chum was yanking on various levers and gear wheels. "Wait a minute!" gasped the young inventor. "I want to throw on the storage battery, and that will give us some light. Then we can see what We are doing." An instant later the whole ship was illuminated, and those aboard her felt calmer. Still the RED CLOUD continued to sink.

"Can't we do something?" yelled Ned. "Start the propellers, Tom!"

"No, I'll use the gas. I can't see where we're heading for, as the searchlight is out of business. We may be in the midst of a lot of bergs. We were flying too low. Just start the gas generating machine."

Ned hurried to obey this order. He saw Tom's object. With the big bag full of gas the airship would settle gently to earth as easily as though under the command of the propellers and wing planes.

In a few minutes the hissing of the machine told that the vapor was being forced into the bag and a little later the downward motion of the ship was checked. She moved more and more slowly toward the earth, until, with a little jar, she settled down, and came to rest. But she was on such an uneven keel that the cabin was tilted at an unpleasant angle.

"Bless my salt-cellar!" cried Mr. Damon. "We are almost standing on our heads!"

"Better that than not standing at all," replied Tom, grimly. "Now to see what the damage is."

He scrambled from the forward door of the cabin, no easy task considering how it was tilted, and the others followed him. It was too dark to note just how much damage had been inflicted, but Tom was relieved to see, as nearly as he could judge, that it was confined to the forward part of the front platform or deck of the ship. The wooden planking was split, but the extent of the break could not be ascertained until daylight. The searchlight connections had been broken by the collision, and it could not be used.

"Now to take a look at the machinery," suggested the young inventor, when he had walked around his craft. "That is what I am worried about more than about the outside."

But, to their joy, they found only a small break in the motor. That was what caused it to stop, and also put the dynamo out of commission.

"We can easily fix that," Tom declared.

"Bless my coffee-spoon!" cried Mr. Damon, who seemed to be running to table accessories in his blessings. Perhaps it was because it was so near supper time. "Bless my coffee-spoon! But how did it happen?"

"We were running too low," declared Tom. "I had forgotten that we were likely to get among tall mountain peaks at any moment, and I set the elevation rudder too low. It was my fault. I should have been on the lookout. We must have struck the mountain of ice a glancing blow, or the result would have been worse than it is. We'll come out of it all right, as it is."

"We can't do anything to-night," observed Ned.

"Only eat," put in Mr. Damon, "and we'll have to take our coffee cups half full, for everything is so tilted that it's like topsy-turvey land. It makes me fairly dizzy!"

But he forgot this in the work of getting a meal, and, though it was prepared under considerable difficulties, at last it was ready.

Bright and early the next morning Tom was up making another inspection of his ship. He found that even if the forward deck was not repaired they could go on, as soon as the motor was in shape, but, as they had some spare wood aboard, it was decided to temporarily repair the smashed platform.

It was cold work, even wearing their thick garments; but, after laboring until their fingers were stiff from the frost, Ned hit on the idea of building a big fire of some evergreen trees near where the ship lay.

"Say, that's all right!" declared Tom, as the warmth of the blaze made itself felt. "We can work better, now!"

The RED CLOUD was tilted on some rough and uneven ground, in among some little hills. On either side arose big peaks, the one in particular that they had hit towering nearly fifteen thousand feet.

Everything was covered with snow and ice, and, in fact, the ice was so thick on the top of the mountains that the crags resembled icebergs rather than stony peaks. The crash of the airship had brought down a great section of this solid rock-ice.

"Do you think we are anywhere near the valley of gold?" asked Mr. Damon that afternoon, when the work was nearly finished.

"It's somewhere in this vicinity." declared Abe. "Me an' my partner passed through jest such a place as this on our way there. I wouldn't wonder but what it wasn't more than a few hundred miles away, now."

"Then we'll soon be there," said Tom. "I'll start in the morning. I could go to-night, but there are a few adjustments I want to make to the motor, and, besides, I think it will be safer, now that we are among these peaks, to navigate in daylight, or at least with the searchlight going. I should have thought of that before."

"Then, if you're not going to start away at once," spoke Mr. Parker, "I think I will walk around a bit, and make some observations. I think we are now in the region where we may expect a movement of the ice. I want to test it, and see if it is traveling in a southerly direction. If it is not now, it will soon be doing that, and the coating of ice may reach even as far as New York."

"Pleasant prospect," murmured Tom. Then he said aloud: "Well if you are going, Mr. Parker, we'll be with you. I'll be glad of the chance to stretch my legs, and what more remains to be done, can be finished in the morning."

Mr. Damon declared that he did not relish a tramp over the ice and snow, and would stay in the warm cabin, but Tom and Ned, with Abe and Mr. Parker started off. The scientist pointed out what he claimed were evidences of the impending movement of the ice, while Abe explained to the lads how the Alaskan Indians of that neighborhood hunted and fished, and how they made huts of blocks of ice.

"We are nearing th' Arctic circle," the old miner said, "and we'll soon be among th' most savage of the Eskimo tribes."

"Is there any hunting around here?" asked Ned.

"Yes, plenty of musk ox," answered Abe.

"I wish I'd brought my gun along and could see one of the big beasts now," went on Ned. He looked anxiously around, but no game was in sight. After a little farther tramp over the icy expanse they all declared that they had seen enough of the dreary landscape, and voted to return to the ship.

As they neared their craft Tom saw several large, shaggy black objects standing in a line on the path the adventurers had come over a little while before. The objects were between the gold-seekers and the RED CLOUD.

"What in the world are those?" asked the young inventor.

"Look to me like black stones," spoke Ned.

"Stones?" cried Abe. "Look out, boys, those are musk oxen; and big ones, too! There's a lot of 'em! Make for the ship! If they attack us we're goners!"

The boys and Mr. Parker needed no second warning. Turning so as to rush past the shaggy creatures, the four headed toward the ship.

But if our friends expected to reach it unmolested they were disappointed. No sooner had they increased their pace than the oxen, with snorts of rage, darted forward. The animals may have imagined they were about to be attacked, and determined to make the first move.

"Here they come!" yelled Ned.

"Sprint for it!" cried Tom.

"Oh, if I only had my gun!" groaned Abe.

It was hard work running over the ice and snow, hampered as they were with their heavy fur garments. They soon realized this, and the pace was telling on them. They were now near to the ship, but the savage creatures still were between them and the craft.

"Try around the other way!" directed Tom, They changed their direction, but the oxen also shifted their ground, and with loud bellows of rage came on, shaking their shaggy heads and big horns, while the hair, hanging down from their sides and flanks, dragged in the snow.

"Right at 'em! Run and yell!" advised the young inventor. "Maybe we can scare 'em!"

They followed his advice. Yelling like Indians the four rushed straight for the animals. For a moment only the creatures halted. Then, bellowing louder than ever they rushed straight at Tom and the others.

The largest of the oxen, with a sudden swerve, made for Mr. Parker, who was slightly in the lead off to one side. In an instant the scientist was tossed high in the air, falling in a snow bank.

"Mr. Damon! Mr. Damon!" yelled Tom, frantically. "Get a gun and shoot these beasts!"

The young inventor and his two companions had come to a halt. The oxen also stopped momentarily. Suddenly Mr. Damon appeared on the deck of the airship. He held two rifles. Laying one down he aimed the other at the ox which was rushing at the prostrate Mr. Parker. The eccentric man fired. He hit the beast on the flank, and, with a bellow of rage it turned.

"Now's our time!" yelled Tom. "Head for the ship, I'll get my electric gun!"

"We can't leave Mr. Parker!" yelled Abe.

But the scientist had arisen, and was running toward the RED CLOUD. He did not seem to be much hurt. Mr. Damon fired again, hitting another beast, but not mortally.

Once more the herd of shaggy creatures came on, but the adventurers were now almost at the ship, on the deck of which stood Mr. Damon, firing as fast as he could work the lever and pull the trigger.

CHAPTER XIX
THE CAVES OF ICE

Keep on firing! Hold 'em back a few minutes and I'll soon turn my electric rifle loose on 'em!" yelled Tom Swift as he sprinted forward. "Keep on shooting, Mr. Damon!"

"Bless my powder-horn! I will!" cried the excited man. "I'll fire all the cartridges there are in the rifle!"

Which, at the rate he was discharging the weapon, would not take a long time. But it had the effect of momentarily checking the advance of the creatures.

Not for long, however. Our friends had barely reached the airship, with Mr. Parker stumbling and slipping on the ice and snow, ere the musk oxen came on again, with loud bellows.

"They're going to charge the ship! They'll ram her!" yelled Ned Newton.

"I think I can stop them!" cried Tom, who had leaped toward his stateroom. He came out a moment later, carrying a peculiar-looking gun, The adventurers had seen it before, but never in operation, as Tom had only put some finishing touches on it since undertaking the voyage to the caves of ice.

"What sort of a weapon is that?" cried Abe, as he helped Mr. Parker on board.

"It's my new electric rifle," answered the young inventor. "I don't know how it will work, as it isn't entirely finished, but I'm going to try it."

Putting it to his shoulder he aimed at the leading musk ox, and pulled a small lever. There was no report, no puff of smoke and no fire, yet the big creature, which had been rushing at the ship, suddenly stopped, swayed for a moment, and then fell over in the snow, kicking in his death agony.

"One down!" yelled Tom. "My rifle works all right, even if it isn't finished!"

He aimed at another ox, and that creature was stopped in its tracks. Mr. Damon had exhausted his cartridges, and had ceased firing, but Abe Abercrombie was ready with his rifle, and opened up on the beasts. Tom killed another with his electric gun, and Abe shot two. This stopped the advance, and only just in time, for the foremost animals were already close to the ship, and had they rushed at the frail hull they might have damaged it beyond repair.

"Here goes for the big one!" cried Tom, and, aiming at the largest ox of the herd, the young inventor pulled the lever. The brute fell over dead, and the rest, terror stricken, turned and fled.

"Hurrah! That's the stuff!" cried Ned Newton, capering about on deck. He had hurried to his stateroom and secured his rifle, and, before the musk oxen were out of sight he had killed one, which gave him great delight.

"Mighty lucky we drove them away," declared Abe. "They are terrible savage at times, an' I reckon we struck one of them times. But say, Tom, what sort of a gun is that you got, anyhow?"

"Oh, it fires electric bullets," explained our hero. "But I haven't time to tell you about it now. Let's get out and skin one of those oxen. The fresh meat will come in good, for we've been living on canned stuff since we left Seattle. We've got time enough before it gets dark."

They hurried to where the shaggy creatures lay in the snow, and soon there was enough fresh meat to last a long time, as it would keep well in the intense cold. Tom put away his electric gun, briefly explaining the system of it to his companions. The time was to come, and that not very far off, when that same electric rifle was to save his life in a remarkable manner, in the wilds of Africa where he went to hunt elephants.

In the cozy cabin that night they sat and talked of the day's adventures. The airship had been slightly lifted up by means of the gas bag, and now rested on a level keel, so it was more comfortable for the gold hunters.

"I did not complete my observations about the great snow slide," remarked Professor Parker, "I trust I will have time to go over the ground again to-morrow."

"We leave early in the morning," objected Tom.

"Besides, I don't believe it would be safe to go over that ground again," put in Mr. Damon.

"Bless my gunpowder! But when I saw those savage creatures rushing at you, I thought it was all up with us. Are you hurt, Parker, my dear fellow? I forgot to ask before."

"Not hurt in the least," answered the scientist. "My heavy and thick fur garments saved me from the beasts' horns, and I fell in some soft snow. I was quite startled for a moment. I thought it might be the beginning of the snow movement."

"It was an ox movement," said Ned, in a low voice to Tom.

Morning saw the travelers again under way, with the Red Cloud now floating high enough to avoid the lofty peaks. The weather was clear but very cold, and Tom, who was in the pilot-house, could see a long distance ahead, and note many towering crags, which, had the airship been flying low enough, would have interfered with her progress.

"We'll have to keep the searchlight going all night, to avoid a collision," he decided.

"Are we anywhere near the place?" asked Mr. Damon.

"We're in th' right region," declared the old miner. "I think we're on th' right track. I recognize a few more landmarks."

"There wouldn't have been any trouble if I hadn't lost the map." complained Tom, bitterly.

"Never mind about that," insisted Abe. "We'll find th' place anyhow. But look ahead there; is that another hail storm headin' this way, Tom?"

The young inventor glanced to where Abe pointed. There was a mist in the air, and, for a time great apprehension was felt, but, in a few minutes there was a violent flurry of snow and they all breathed easier. For, though the flakes were so numerous as to completely shut off the view, there was no danger to the airship from them. Tom steered by the compass.

The storm lasted several hours, and when it was over the adventurers found themselves several miles nearer their destination--at least they hoped they were nearer it, for they were going it blind.

Abe declared they were now in the region of the gold valley. They cruised about for two days, making vain observations by means of powerful telescopes, but they saw no signs of any depression which corresponded with the place whence Abe had seen the gold taken from. At times they passed over Indian villages, and had glimpses of the skin-clad inhabitants rushing out to point to the strange sight of the airship overhead. Tom was beginning to reproach himself again for his carelessness in losing the map, and it did begin to took as if they were making a fruitless search.

Still they all kept up their good spirits, and Mr. Damon concocted some new dishes from the meat of the musk oxen. It was about a week after the fight with the savage creatures when, one day, as Ned was on duty in the pilothouse, he happened to lock down. What he saw caused him to call to Tom.

"What's the matter?" demanded the young inventor, as he hurried forward.

"Look down there," directed Ned. "It looks as if we were sailing over a lot of immense beehives of the old-fashioned kind."

Tom looked. Below were countless, rounded hummocks of snow or ice. Some were very large--as immense as a great shed in which a dirigible balloon could be housed--while others were as small as the ice huts in which the Eskimos live.

"That's rather strange," remarked Tom. "I wonder--"

But he did not complete his sentence, for Abe Abercrombie, who had come to stand beside him, suddenly yelled out:

"The caves of ice! The caves of ice! Now I know where we are! We're close to the valley of gold! There are the caves of ice, and just beyond is th' place we're lookin' for! We've found it at last!"

CHAPTER XX
IN THE GOLD VALLEY

The excited cries of the old miner brought Mr. Damon and Mr. Parker to the pilothouse on the run.

"Bless my refrigerator!" exclaimed Mr. Damon. "Are there more of those savage, shaggy creatures down there?"

"No, but we are over th' caves of ice," explained Abe. "That means we are near th' gold."

"You don't say so!" burst out the scientist. "The caves of ice! Now I can begin my real observations! I have a theory that the caves are on top of a strata of ice that is slowly moving down, and will eventually bury the whole of the North American continent. Let me once get down there, and I can prove what I say."

"I'd a good deal rather you wouldn't prove it, if it's going to be anything like it was on Earthquake Island, or out among the diamond makers." said Tom Swift. "But we will go down there, to see what they are like. Perhaps there is a trail from among the ice caves to the valley of gold."

"I don't think so," said Abe, shaking his head.

"I think th' gold valley lies over that high ridge," and he pointed to one. "That's where me an' my partner was," he went on. "I recognize th' place now."

"Well, we'll go down here, anyhow," decided Tom, and he pulled the lever to let some gas out of the bag, and tilted the deflection rudder to send the airship toward the odd caves.

And, curious enough did our friends find them when they had made a landing and got out to walk about them. It was very cold, for on every side was solid ice. They walked on ice, which was like a floor beneath their feet, level save where the ice caves reared themselves. As for the caverns, they, too, were hollowed out of the solid ice. It was exactly as though there had once been a level surface of some liquid. Then by some upheaval of nature, the surface was blown into bubbles, some large and some small. Then the whole thing had frozen solid, and the bubbles became hollow caves. In time part of the sides fell in and made an opening, so that nearly all the caves were capable of being entered.

This method of their formation was advanced as a theory by Mr. Parker, and no one cared to dispute him. The gold-seekers walked about, gazing on the ice caves with wonder showing on their faces.

It was almost like being in some fantastic scene from fairyland, the big ice bubbles representing the houses, the roofs being rounded like the igloos of the Eskimos. Some had no means of entrance, the outer surface showing no break. Others had small openings, like a little doorway, while of still others there remained but a small part of the original cave, some force of nature having crumbled and crushed it.

"Wonderful! Wonderful!" exclaimed Mr. Parker. "It bears out my theory exactly! Now to see how fast the ice is moving."

"How are you going to tell?" asked Tom.

"By taking some mark on this field of ice, and observing a distant peak. Then I will set up a stake, and by noting their relative positions, I can tell just how fast the ice field is moving southward." The scientist hurried into the ship to get a sharpened stake he had prepared for this purpose.

"How fast do you think the ice is moving?" asked Ned.

"Oh, perhaps two or three feet a year." "Two or three feet a year?" gasped Mr. Damon. "Why, Parker, my dear fellow, at that rate it will be some time before the ice gets to New York."

"Oh, yes. I hardly expect it will reach there within two thousand years, but my theory will be proved, just the same!"

"Humph!" exclaimed Abe Abercrombie, "I ain't goin' to worry any more, if it's goin' t' take all that while. I reckoned, to hear him talk, that it was goin' t' happen next summer."

"So did I," agreed Tom, but their remarks were lost on Mr. Parker who was busy making observations. The young inventor and the others walked about among the ice caves.

"Some of these caverns would be big enough to house the RED CLOUD in case of another hail storm," observed Tom. "That one over there would hold two craft the size of mine," and, in fact, probably three could have gotten in if the opening had been somewhat enlarged, for the ice cave to which our hero pointed was an immense one.

As the adventurers were walking about they were startled by a terrific crashing sound. They started in alarm, for, off to their left, the top of one of the ice caverns had crashed inward, the blocks of frozen water crushing and grinding against one another.

"It's a good thing we weren't in there," remarked Tom, and he could not repress a shudder, "There wouldn't have been much left of the RED CLOUD if she had been inside."

It was a desolate place, in spite of the wild beauty of it, and beautiful it was when the sun shone on the ice caves, making them sparkle as if they were studded with diamonds. But it was cold and cheerless, and there were no signs that human beings had ever been there. Mr. Parker had completed the setting of his stake, and picked out his landmarks, and was gravely making his "observations," and jotting down some figures in a notebook.

"How fast is it moving, Parker?" called Mr. Damon.

"I can't tell yet," was the response. "It will require observations extending over several days before I will know the rate."

"Then we might as well go on," suggested Tom. "There is nothing to be gained from staying here, and I would like to get to the gold valley. Abe says we are near it."

"Right over that ridge, I take it to be," replied the miner. "An' we can't get there any too soon for me. Those Fogers may git their ship fixed up, an' arrive before we do if we wait much longer."

"Not much danger, I guess," declared Ned.

"Well, we'll go up in the air, and see what we can find," decided Tom, as he turned back toward the ship.

They found the "ridge" as Abe designated it, to be a great plateau, over a hundred miles in extent, and they were the better part of that day crossing it, for they went slowly, so as not to miss the valley which the miner was positive was close at hand. Mr. Parker disliked leaving the ice caves, but Abe said there were more in the valley where they were going, and the scientist could renew his observations.

It was getting dusk when Tom, who was peering through a powerful glass, called out:

"Well, we're at the end of the plateau, and it seems to dip down into a valley just beyond here."

"Then that's the place!" cried Abe, excitedly. "Go slow, Tom."

Our hero needed no such caution. Carefully he sent the airship forward. A few minutes later they were passing over a large Eskimo village, the fur-clad inhabitants of which rushed about wildly excited at the sight of the airship.

"There they are! Them's th' beggars!" cried the old miner. "Them's th' fellows who drove me an' my partner away. But there's th' valley of gold! I know it now! How t' fill our pockets with nuggets!"

"Are you sure this is the place?" asked Mr. Damon.

"Sartin sure of it!" declared Abe. "Put her down, Tom! Put her down!"

"All right," agreed the young inventor, as he shifted the deflection rudder. The airship began her descent into the valley. The edge of the plateau, leading down into the great depression was now black with the Eskimos and Indians, who were capering about, gesticulating wildly.

"It's quite a surprise party to 'em," observed Ned Newton.

"Yes, I hope they don't spring one on us," added Tom.

Down and down went the RED CLOUD lower and lower into the valley.

"There are ice caves there!" cried Mr. Parker, pointing to the curiously rounded and hollow hummocks. "Lots of them!"

"And larger than the others!" added Mr. Damon.

The airship was now moving slowly, for Tom wanted to pick out a good landing place. He saw a smooth stretch of the ice just ahead of him, in front of an immense ice cave.

"I'll make for that," he told Ned.

A few minutes later the craft had come to rest. Tom shut off the power and hurried from the pilothouse, donning his fur coat as he rushed out. A blast of frigid air met him as he opened the outer door of the cabin. Back on the ridge of the plateau he could see the fringe of Indians.

"Well, we're here in the valley," he said, as his friends gathered about him on the icy ground.

"An' now for th' gold!" cried Abe, "for it's here that th' nuggets are--enough for all of us! Come on an' have a hunt for 'em!"

CHAPTER XXI
THE FOGERS ARRIVE

In Spite of the fact that he tried to remain calm, Tom Swift felt a wild exultation as he thought of what lay before him and his friends. To be in a place where gold could be picked up! where they might all become fabulously wealthy! where the ground might be seen covered with the precious yellow metal! this was enough to set the nerves of any one a-tingle!

Tom could hardly realize it at first. After many hardships, no little danger, and after an attempt on the part of their enemies to defeat them, they had at last reached their goal. Now, as Abe had said, they could hunt for the gold.

But if they expected to see the precious yellow nuggets lying about ready to be picked up like so many kernels of corn, they were disappointed. A quick look all about showed them only a vast extent of ice and snow, broken here and there by the big caves of ice. There were not so many of the latter as at the first place they stopped, but the caverns were larger.

"Gold--I don't see any gold," remarked Ned Newton, with a disappointed air. "Where is it?"

"Bless my pocketbook, yes! Where is it?" demanded Mr. Damon.

"Oh, we've got to dig for it," explained Abe. "It's only when there's been a slight thaw that some of th' pebble nuggets kin be seen. They're under th' ice, an' we've got t' dig for 'em."

"Does it ever thaw up here?" asked Mr. Parker. "The ice of the caves seems thick enough to last forever."

"It does thaw an' melt some," went on the miner. "But some of th' caves last all through what they call 'summer' up here, though it's more like winter. We're above th' Arctic circle now, friends."

"Maybe we can keep on to the Pole," suggested Ned.

"Not this trip," spoke Tom, grimly. "We'll try for the gold, first."

"Yes, an' I'm goin' t' begin diggin' right away!" exclaimed Abe, as he turned back into the airship, and came out again with a pick and shovel, a supply of which implements had been brought along. The others followed his example, and soon the ice chips were flying about in a shower, while the sun shining on them gave the appearance of a rainbow.

"Look at those Indians watching us," remarked Ned to Tom, as he paused in his chipping of the frozen surface. The young inventor glanced up toward the distant plateau where a fringe of dark figures stood. The natives were evidently intently watching the gold-seekers.

"Do you think there's any danger from them. Abe?" asked Tom.

"Not much," was the reply. "They made trouble for me an' my partner, but I guess th' airship has scared 'em sufficient, so they won't come snoopin' down here," and Abe fell to at his digging again.

Mr. Damon was also vigorously wielding a pick, but Mr. Parker like the true scientist he was, had renewed his observations. Evidently the gold had no attractions for him, or, if it did, he preferred to wait until he had finished his calculations.

Vigorously the adventurers wielded their implements, making the ice fly, but for an hour or more no gold was discovered. Mr. Damon, after picking lightly at a certain place, would get discouraged, and move on to another. So did Ned, and Tom, after going down quite a way, left off work, and walked over to one of the big ice caves.

"What's up?" asked Ned, resting from his labors.

"I was thinking whether it would be safe to put the RED CLOUD in this ice cave for a shelter," replied Tom. "There may come up a hail storm at any time, and damage it. The caves would be just the place for it, only I'm afraid the roof might collapse."

"It looks strong," said Ned. "Let's ask Mr. Parker his opinion."

"Good idea," agreed Tom.

The scientist was soon taking measurements of the thickness of the cave roof, noting its formation, and looking at the frozen floor.

"I see no reason why this cave should collapse," he finally announced. "The only danger is the movement of the whole valley of ice, and that is too gradual to cause any immediate harm. Yes, I think the airship could be housed in the ice cave."

"Then I'll run her in, and she'll be safer," decided Tom. "I guess we three can do it, Ned, and leave Mr. Damon and Abe to keep on digging for gold." The airship was so buoyant that it could easily be moved about on the bicycle wheels on which it rested, and soon, after the lower edge of the opening into the ice cave had been smoothed down, the RED CLOUD was placed in the novel shelter.

"Now to continue the search for the yellow nuggets!" cried Ned, and Tom went with him, even Mr. Parker condescending to take a pick, now. Abe was the only one who dug steadily in one place. The others tried spot after spot.

"You've got t' stick t' one lead until you find somethin', or until it peters out," explained the miner. "You must git down to th' dirt before you'll find any gold, though you may strike a few grains that have worked up into th' ice."

After this advice they all kept to one hole until they had worked down through the ice to the dirt surface below. But even then, Abe, who was the first to achieve this, found no gold, and the old miner went to another location.

All the rest of that day they dug, but with no result. Not even a few grains of yellow dust rewarded their efforts.

"Are you sure this is the right place?" asked Mr. Damon, somewhat fretfully, of Abe, as they ate supper that night in the airship, sheltered as it was in the ice cave.

"I'm positive of it," was the reply. "There's gold here, but it will take some prospectin' t' find it. Maybe th' deposits have been shifted by th' ice movement, as Mr. Parker says. But it's here, an' we'll git it. We'll try ag'in t'-morrow."

They did try, but with small success. Laboring all day in the cold the only result was a few little yellow pebbles that Tom found imbedded in the ice. But they were gold, and the finding of them gave the seekers hope as they wearily began their task the following day. The weather seemed even colder, and there was the indication of a big storm.

They were scattered in different places on the ice, not far away from the big cave, each one picking away vigorously. Suddenly Abe, who had laboriously worked his way down to the dirt, gave an exultant yell.

"I've struck it! Struck it rich!" he shouted, leaping about as he threw down his pick, "Look here, everybody!" He stooped down over the hole. They all ran to his side, and saw him lifting from a little pocket in the dirt, several large, yellow pebbles.

"Gold! Gold!" cried Abe. "We've struck it at last!"

For a moment no one spoke, though there was a wild beating of their hearts. Then, off toward the farther end of the valley there sounded a curious noise. It was a shouting and yelling, mingled with the snapping of whips and the howls and barkings of dogs.

"Bless my handkerchief!" cried Mr. Damon. "What's that?"

They all saw a moment later. Approaching over the frozen snow were several Eskimo sledges, drawn by dog teams, and the native drivers were shouting and cracking their whips of walrus hide.

"The natives are coming to attack us!" cried Ned.

Tom said nothing. He was steadily observing the approaching sleds. They came on rapidly. Abe was holding the golden nuggets in his gloved hands.

"Get the guns! Where's your electric rifle, Tom?" cried Mr. Damon.

"I don't believe we'll need the guns--just yet," answered the young inventor, slowly.

"Bless my cartridge-belt! Why not?" demanded the eccentric man.

"Because those are the Fogers," replied Tom. "They have followed us--Andy and his father! Andy Foger here!" gasped Ned.

Tom nodded grimly. A few minutes later the sleds had come to a halt not far from our friends, and Andy, followed by his father, leaped off his conveyance. The two were clad in heavy fur garments.

"Ha, Tom Swift! You didn't get here much ahead of us!" exulted the bully. "I told you I'd get even with you! Come on, now, dad, we'll get right to work digging for gold!"

Tom and his companions did not know what to say.

CHAPTER XXII
JUMPING THE CLAIM

There was a sneering look on Andy's face, and Mr. Foger, too, seemed delighted at having reached the valley of gold almost as soon as had our friends. Tom and the others looked at the means by which the bully had arrived. There were four sleds, each one drawn by seven dogs, and in charge of a dark-skinned native. On the two foremost sleds Andy and his father had ridden, while the other two evidently contained their supplies.

For a moment Andy surveyed Tom's party and then, turning to one of the native drivers, he said:

"We'll camp here. You fellows get to work and make an ice house, and some of you cook a meal--I'm hungry."

"No need build ice house," replied the native, who spoke English brokenly.

"Why not?" demanded Andy.

"Live in ice cave-plenty much ob'em--plenty much room," went on the Eskimo, indicating several of the large caverns.

"Ha! That's a good idea," agreed Mr. Foger, "Andy, my son, we have houses already made for us, and very comfortable they seem, too. We'll take up our quarters in one, and then hunt for the gold."

Mr. Foger seemed to ignore Tom and his friends. Abe Abercrombie strode forward.

"Look here, you Fogers!" he exclaimed without ceremony, "was you calculatin' on stakin' any claims here?"

"If you mean are we going to dig for gold, we certainly are," replied Andy insolently, "and you can't stop us."

"I don't know about that," went on Abe, grimly. "I ain't goin' t' say nothin' now, about th' way you stole th' map from me, an' made a copy, but I am goin t' say this, an' that is it won't be healthy fer any of you t' git in my way, or t' try t' dig on our claims!"

"We'll dig where we please!" cried Andy. "You don't own this valley!"

"We own as much of it as we care to stake out, by right of prior discovery!" declared Tom, firmly.

"And I say we'll dig where we please!" insisted Andy. "Hand me a pick," he went on to another of the natives.

"Wait jest a minute," spoke Abe calmly, as he put his little store of nuggets in the pocket of his fur coat, and drew out a big revolver. "It ain't healthy t' talk that way, Andy Foger, an' th' sooner you find that out th' better. You ain't in Shopton now, an' th' only law here is what we make for ourselves. Tom, maybe you'd better get out th' rifles, an' your electric gun, after all. It seems like we might have trouble," and Abe cooly looked to see if his weapon was loaded.

"Oh, of course we didn't mean to usurp any of your rights, my dear friend!" exclaimed Mr. Foger quickly, and he seemed nervous at the sight of the big revolver, while Andy hastily moved until he was behind the biggest of the sledge drivers. "We don't want to violate any of your rights," went on Mr. Foger. "But this valley is large, and do I understand that you claim all of it?"

"We could if we wanted to," declared Abe stoutly; "but we'll be content with three-quarter of it, seein' we was here fust. If you folks want t' dig fer gold, go over there," and he pointed to a spot some distance away.

"We'll dig where we please!" cried Andy.

"Oh, will you?" and there was an angry light in Abe's eyes. "I guess, Tom, you'd better git--"

"No! No! My son is wrong--he is too hasty," interposed Mr. Foger. "We will go away--certainly we will. The valley is large enough for both of us--just as you say. Come, Andy!"

The bully seemed about to refuse, but a look at Abe's angry face and a sight of Mr. Damon coming from the cave where the airship was, with a rifle, for the eccentric man had hastened to get his weapon--this sight calmed Andy down. Without further words he and his father got back on their sleds, and were soon being driven off to where a large ice cave loomed up, about a mile away.

"Good riddance," muttered the miner, "now we kin go on diggin' without bein' bothered by that little scamp."

"I don't know about that," spoke Tom, shaking his head dubiously. "There's always trouble when Andy Foger's within a mile. I'm afraid we haven't seen the last of him."

"He'd better not come around here ag'in," declared Abe. "Queer, how he should turn up, jest when I made a big strike."

"They must have come on all the way from where their airship was wrecked, by means of dog sleds," observed Ned, and the others agreed with him. Later they learned that this was so; that after the accident to the ANTHONY, the crew had refused to proceed farther north, and had gone back. But Mr. Foger had hired the natives with the dog teams, and, by means of the copy of the map and with what knowledge his Eskimos had, had reached the valley of gold.

"We have certainly struck it rich," went on Abe, as he went back to where he had dug the hole. "Now we'd better all begin prospectin' here, for it looks like a big deposit. We'll stake out a large enough claim to take it all in. I guess Mr. Parker can do that, seein' as how he knows about such things."

The scientist agreed to do this part of the work, it being understood that all the gold discovered would be shared equally after the expenses of the trip had been paid.

Feverishly Abe and the others began to dig. They did not come upon such a rich deposit as the miner had found, but there were enough nuggets picked up to prove that the expedition would be very successful.

No more attention was paid to the Fogers, but through the telescope Tom could see that the bully and his father had made a camp in one of the ice caves, and that both were eagerly digging in the frozen surface of the valley.

Before night several thousand dollars' worth of gold had been taken out by our friends. It was stored in the airship, and then, after suppers the craft's searchlight was taken off, and placed in such a position in front of the cave of ice so that the beams would illuminate the claim staked out by Tom and the others.

"We'll stand watch an' watch," suggested Abe, "but I don't think them Fogers will come around here ag'in."

They did not, and the night passed peacefully. The next day our friends were again at work digging for gold. So were the Fogers, as could be observed through the glass, but it was impossible to see whether they got any nuggets.

The gold seemed to be in "pockets," and that day the ones in the vicinity of the strike first made by Abe were cleaned out.

"We'll have to locate some new 'pockets,'" said the miner, and the adventurers scattered over the frozen plain to look for other deposits of the precious metal.

Tom and Ned were digging together not far from one another. Suddenly Ned let out a joyful cry.

"Strike anything?" asked Tom.

"Something rich," answered the bank clerk. He lifted from a hole in the ground a handful of the golden pebbles.

"It's as good as Abe's was!" exclaimed Tom. "We must stake it out at once, or the Fogers may jump it. Come on, we'll go back and tell Abe, and get Mr. Parker and Mr. Damon over here."

The three men were some distance away, and there was no sign of the Fogers. Tom and Ned hurried back to where their friends were, leaving their picks and shovels on the frozen ground.

The good news was soon told, and, with some stakes hastily made from some extra wood carried on the airship, the little party hastened back to where Tom and Ned had made their strike.

As they emerged from behind a big hummock of ice they saw, standing over the holes which the lads had dug, Andy Foger and his father! Each one had a rifle, and there was a smile of triumph on Andy's face!

"What are you doing here?" cried Tom, the hot blood mounting to his cheeks.

"We've just staked out a claim here," answered the bully.

"And you deserted it," put in Mr. Foger smoothly. "I think your mining friend will tell you that we have a right to take up an abandoned claim."

"But we didn't abandon it!" declared Tom. "We only went away to get the stakes."

"The claim was abandoned, and we have 'jumped' it," went on Mr. Foger, and he cocked his rifle. "I need hardly tell you that possession is nine points of the law, and that we intend to remain. Andy, is your gun loaded?"

"Yes, pa."

"I--I guess they've got us--fer th' time bein'," murmured Abe, as he motioned to Tom and the others to come away. "Besides they've got guns, an' we haven't--but wait," added the miner, mysteriously. "I haven't played all my tricks yet."

CHAPTER XXIII
ATTACKED BY NATIVES

To state that Tom and his friends were angry at the trick the Fogers had played on them would be putting it mildly. There was righteous indignation in their hearts, and, as for the young inventor he felt that much blame was attached to him for his neglect in not remaining on guard at the place of the lucky strike while Ned went to call the others.

"I guess Andy must have been spying on us," spoke Ned, "or he would never have known when to rush up just as he did; as soon as we left."

"Probably," admitted Tom, bitterly.

"But, bless my penholder!" cried Mr. Damon. "Can't we do something, Abe? Won't the law--?"

"There ain't any law out here, except what you make yourself," said the miner. "I guess they've got us for th' time bein'."

"What do you mean by that?" asked Tom, detecting a gleam of hope in Abe's tone.

"Well, I mean that I think we kin git ahead of 'em. Come on back to th' ship, an' we'll talk it over."

They walked away, leaving Andy and his father in possession of the rich deposits of gold, and that it was much richer even then than the hole Abe had first discovered was very evident. The two Fogers were soon at work, digging out the yellow metal with the pick and shovels Tom and Ned had so thoughtlessly dropped.

"What little law there is out here they've got on their side," went on Abe, "an' they've got possession, too, which is more. Of course we could go at 'em in a pitched battle, but I take it you don't want any bloodshed?" and he looked at Tom.

"Of course not," replied the lad quickly, "but I'd like to meet Andy alone, with nothing but my fists for a little while," and Tom's eyes snapped.

"So would I," added Ned.

"Perhaps we can find another pocket of gold better than that one," suggested Mr. Damon.

"We might," admitted Abe, "but that one was ours an' we're entitled to it. This valley is rich in gold deposits, but you can't allers put your hand on 'em. We may have t' hunt around for a week until we strike another. An', meanwhile, them Fogers will be takin' our gold! It's not to be borne! I'll find some way of drivin' 'em out. An' we've got t' do it soon, too."

"You mean if we don't that they'll get all the gold?" asked Mr. Damon.

"No, I mean that soon it will be th' long night up here, an' we can't work. We'll have t' go back, an' I don't want t' go back until I've made my pile."

"Neither do any of us, I guess," spoke Tom, "but there doesn't seem to be any help for it."

They discussed several plans on reaching the ship, but none seemed feasible without resorting to force, and this they did not want to do, as they feared there might be bloodshed. When night closed in they could see the gleam of a campfire, kindled by the Foger party, at the gold-pocket, from bits of the scrubby trees that grew in that frigid clime.

"They're going to stay on guard," announced Tom. "We can't get it away from them to-night."

Though Abe had spoken of some plan to regain the advantage the Fogers had of them, the old miner was not quite ready to propose it. All the next day he seemed very thoughtful, while going about with the others, seeking new deposits of gold. Luck did not seem to be with them. They found two or three places where there were traces of the yellow pebbles, but in no very great quantity.

Meanwhile the Fogers were busy at the pocket Ned had located. They seemed to be taking out much of the precious metal.

"And it all ought to be ours," declared Tom, bitterly.

"Yes, and it shall be, too!" suddenly exclaimed. Abe. "I think I have a plan that will beat 'em."

"What is it?" asked Tom.

"Let's get back to the ship, and I'll tell you," said Abe. "We can't tell when one of their natives might be sneakin' in among these ice caves, an' they understand some English. They might give my scheme away."

In brief Abe's plan, as he unfolded it in the cabin of the RED CLOUD was this:

They would divide into two parties, one consisting of Ned and Tom, and the other of the three men. The latter, by a circuitous route, would go to the ice caves where the Fogers had established their camp. It was there that the Indians remained during the day, while Andy and his father labored at the gold pocket, for, after the first day when they had had the natives aid them, father and son had worked alone at the hole, probably fearing to trust the Indians. At night, though either Andy or his father remained on guard, with one or two of the dusky-skinned dog drivers.

"But we'll work this trick before night," said Abe. "We three men will get around to where the natives are in the ice cave. We'll pretend to attack them, and raise a great row, firing our guns in the air, and all that sort of thing, an' yellin' t' beat th' band. Th' natives will yell, too, you can depend on that."

"Th' Fogers will imagine we are tryin' t' git away with their sleds an' supplies, an' maybe their gold, if they've got it stored in th' ice cave. Naturally Andy or his father will run here, an' that will leave only one on guard at th' mine. Then Tom an' Ned can sneak up. Th' two of 'em will be a match for even th' old Foger, if he happens t' stay, an' while Tom or Ned comes up in front, t' hold his attention, th' other can come up in back, an' grab his arms, if he tries t' shoot. Likely Andy will remain at th' gold hole, an' you two lads kin handle him, can't you?"

"Well, I guess!" exclaimed Tom and Ned together.

The plan worked like a charm. Abe, Mr. Damon and Mr. Parker raised a great din at the ice cave where the Foger natives were. The sound carried to the hole where Andy and his father were digging out the gold. Mr. Foger at once ran toward the cave, while Andy, catching up his gun, remained on the alert.

Then came the chance of Tom and Ned. The latter coming from his hiding-place, advanced boldly toward the bully, while Tom, making a detour, worked his way up behind.

"Here! You keep away!" cried Andy, catching sight of Ned. "I see what the game is, now! It's a trick!"

"You're a nice one to talk about tricks!" declared Ned, advancing slowly.

"Keep away if you don't want to get hurt!" yelled Andy.

"Oh, you wouldn't hurt me; would you?" mocked Ned, who wanted to give Tom time to sneak up behind the bully.

"Yes, I would! Keep back!" Andy was nervously fingering his weapon. The next instant his gun flew from his grasp, and he went over backward in Tom's strong grip; for the young inventor, in his sealskin shoes had worked up in the rear without a sound. The next moment Andy broke away and was running for his life, leaving Tom and Ned in possession of the gold hole, and that without a shot being fired. A little later the three men, who had hurried away from the cave as Mr. Foger rushed up to see what caused the racket, joined Tom and Ned, and formal possession was taken of their lucky strike.

"We'll guard it well, now," decided Tom, and later that day they moved some supplies near the hole, and for a shelter built an igloo, Eskimo fashion, in which work Abe had had some experience. Then they moved the airship to another ice cave, nearer their "mine" as they called it, and prepared to stand guard.

But there seemed to be no need, for the following day there was no trace of the Fogers. They and their natives had disappeared.

"I guess we were too much for them," spoke Tom. But the sequel was soon to prove differently.

It was three days after our friends had regained their mine, during which time they had dug out considerable gold, that toward evening, as Tom was taking the last of the output of yellow pebbles into the cave where the airship was, he looked across the valley.

"Looks like something coming this way," observed the young inventor. "Natives, I guess."

"It is," agreed Ned, "quite a large party, too!"

"Better tell Abe and the others," went on Tom. "I don't like the looks of this. Maybe the sudden disappearance of the Fogers has something to do with it."

Abe, Mr. Damon and Mr. Parker hurried from the ice cave. They had caught up their guns as they ran out.

"They're still coming on," called Tom, "and are headed this way."

"They're Indians, all right!" exclaimed Abe. "Hark! What's that?"

It was the sound of shouting and singing.

Through the gathering dusk the party advanced. Our friends closely scanned them. There was something familiar about the two leading figures, and it could now be seen that in the rear were a number of dog sleds.

"There's Andy Foger and his father!" cried Ned. "They've gone and got a lot of Eskimos to help them drive us away."

"That's right!" admitted Tom. "I guess we're in for it now!"

With a rush the natives, led by the Fogers, came on. They were yelling now. An instant later they began firing their guns.

"It's a fierce attack!" cried Tom. "Into the ice cave for shelter! We can cover the gold mine from there. I'll get my electric gun!"

CHAPTER XXIV
THE WRECK OF THE AIRSHIP

Almost before our friends could retreat into the cave which now sheltered the RED CLOUD, the attacking natives opened fire. Fortunately they only had old-fashioned, muzzle-loading muskets, and, as their aim was none of the best, there was comparatively little danger. The bullets, however, did sing through the fast-gathering darkness with a vicious sound, and struck the heavy sides and sloping front of the ice cave with a disconcerting "ping!"

"I don't hear Andy or his father firing!" called Tom, as he and the others returned the fire of the savage Indians. "I could tell their guns by the sharper reports. The Fogers carry repeating rifles, and they're fine ones, if they're anything like the one we took from Andy, Ned."

"That's right," agreed Tom's chum, "I don't believe Andy or his father dare fire. They're afraid to, and they're putting the poor ignorant natives up to it. Probably they hired them to try to drive us away."

This, as they afterward learned, was exactly the case.

The battle, if such it could be called, was kept up. There was about a hundred natives, all of whom had guns, and, though they were slow to load, there were enough weapons to keep up a constant fusilade. On their part, Tom and the others fired at first over the heads of the natives, for they did not want to kill any of the deluded men. Later, though, when they saw the rush keeping up, they fired at their legs, and disabled several of the Eskimos, the electric gun proving very effective.

It was now quite dark, and the firing slackened. From their position in the cave, Tom and the others could command the hole where the gold was, and, as they saw several natives sneaking up to it the young inventor and Ned, both of whom were good shots, aimed to have the bullets strike the ice close to where the Indians were.

This sort of shooting was enough, and the natives scurried away. Then Tom hit on the plan of playing the searchlight on the spot, and this effectually prevented an unseen attack. It seemed to discourage the enemy, too for they did not venture into that powerful glow of light.

"They won't do anything more until morning," declared Abe. "Then we'll have it hot an' heavy, though, I'm afeered. Well, we'll have t' make th' best of it!"

They took turns standing guard that night, but no attack was made. The fact of the Fogers coming back with the band of Indians told Tom, more plainly than words, how desperately his enemies would do battle with them. Anxiously they waited for the morning.

Several times in the night Mr. Parker was seen roaming about uneasily, though it was not his turn to be on guard. Finally Tom asked him what was the matter, and if he could not sleep.

"It isn't that," answered the scientist, "but I am worried about the ice. I can detect a slight but peculiar movement by means of some of my scientific instruments. I am alarmed about it. I fear something is going to happen."

But Tom was too worried about the outcome of the fight he knew would be renewed on the next day, to think much about the ice movement. He thought it would only be some scientific phenomena that would amount to little.

With the first streak of the late dawn, the gold-seekers were up, and partook of a hot breakfast, with strong coffee which Mr. Damon brewed. Tom took an observation from the mouth of the cave. The searchlight was still dimly glowing, and it did not disclose anything. Tom turned it off. He thought he saw a movement among the ranks of the enemy, who had camped just beyond the gold hole.

"I guess they're coming!" cried the lad. "Get ready for them!"

The adventurers caught up their guns, and hurried to the entrance of the cave. Mr. Parker lingered behind, and was observed to be narrowly scanning the walls of the cavern.

"Come on, Parker, my dear man!" begged Mr. Damon. "We are in grave danger, and we need your help. Bless my life insurance policy! but I never was in such a state as this."

"We may soon be in a worse one," was the answer of the gloomy scientist.

"What do you mean?" asked Mr. Damon, but he hurried on without waiting for a reply.

Suddenly, from without the cave came a series of fierce yells. It was the battle-cry of the Indians. At the same moment there sounded a fusillade of guns.

"The battle is beginning!" cried Tom Swift, grimly. He held his electric gun, though he had not used it very much in the previous attack, preferring to save it for a time of more need.

As the defenders of the cave reached the entrance they saw the body of natives rushing forward. They were almost at the gold hole, with Andy Foger and his father discreetly behind the first row of Eskimos, when, with a suddenness that was startling, there sounded throughout the whole valley a weird sound!

It was like the wailing of some giant--the sighing of some mighty wind. At the same time the air suddenly became dark, and then there came a violent snow squall, shutting out instantly the sight of the advancing natives. Tom and the others could not see five feet beyond the cave.

"This will delay the attack," murmured Ned, "They can't see to come at us."

Mr. Parker came running up from the interior of the cave. On his face there was a look of alarm.

"We must leave here at once!" he cried.

"Leave here?" repeated Tom. "Why must we? The enemy are out there! We'd run right into them!"

"It must be done!" insisted the scientist. "We must leave the cave at once!"

"What for?" cried Mr. Damon.

"Because the movement of the ice that I predicted, has begun. It is much more rapid than I supposed it would be. In a short time this cave and all the others will be crushed flat!"

"Crushed flat!" gasped Tom.

"Yes, the caves of ice are being destroyed! Hark! You can hear them snapping!"

They all listened. Above the roar of the storm could be made out the noise of crushing, grinding ice-sounds like cannon being fired, as the great masses of frozen crystal snapped like frail planks.

"The ice caves are being destroyed by an upheaval of nature!" went on Mr. Parker. "This one will soon go! The walls are bulging now! We must get out!"

"But the natives! They will kill us!" cried Mr. Damon. "Bless my soul! what a trying position to be in."

"I guess the natives are as bad off as we are," suggested Ned. "They're not firing, and I can hear cries of alarm, I think they're running away."

There was a lull in the snow flurry, and the white curtain seemed to lift for a moment. The gold-seekers had a glimpse of the natives in full retreat, with the Fogers--father and son--racing panic-stricken after them. Tom could also see a big cave, just beyond the gold hole, collapse and crumble to pieces like a house of cards.

"We have no time to lose!" Mr. Parker warned them. "The roof of this cave is slowly coming down. The sides are collapsing! We must get out!"

"Then wheel out the airship!" cried Tom. "We must save that! We needn't fear the natives, now!"

The young inventor hurried to the RED CLOUD calling to Ned and the others. They hastened to his side. It was an easy matter to move the airship along on the wheels. It neared the opening of the cave. The rumbling, roaring, grinding sound of the ice increased.

"Why--why!" cried Tom in surprise and alarm, as the craft neared the mouth of the ice cavern, "we can't get it out--the opening is too small! Yet it came in easily enough!"

"The cave is collapsing--growing smaller every moment!" cried Mr. Parker. "We have only time to save our lives! Run out!"

"And leave the airship? Never!" yelled Tom.

"You must! You can't save that and your life!"

"Get axes and make the opening bigger!" suggested Ned, who, like his chum, could not bear to think of the destruction of the beautiful craft.

"No time! No time!" shouted Mr. Parker, frantically, "We must get out! Save what you can from the ship--the gold--some supplies--the guns--some food--save what you can!"

Then ensued a wild effort to get from the doomed craft what they could--what they would need if they were to save their lives in that cold and desolate country. Food, some blankets--their guns--as much of the gold as they could hastily gather together--their weapons and some ammunition--all this was carried from the cabin outside the cave. The entrance was rapidly growing smaller. The roof was already pressing down on the gas-bag.

Tom gave one last look at his fine craft. There were tears in his eyes. He started into the cabin for something he had forgotten. Mr. Parker grabbed him by the arm.

"Don't go in!" he cried hoarsely. "The cave will collapse in another instant!" He rushed with Tom out of the cavern, and not a moment too soon. The others were already outside.

Then with a rush and a roar, with a sound like a great explosion, with a rending, grinding and booming as the great pieces of ice collapsed one against the other, the big ice cave settled in, as does some great building when the walls are weakened!

Down crashed the roof of the ice cave! Down upon the RED CLOUD, burying out of sight, forever, under thousands of tons of ice and snow, the craft which was the pride of Tom Swift's heart! It was the end of the airship!

Tom felt a moisture of tears in his eyes as he stood there in the midst of the snowstorm.

CHAPTER XXV
THE RESCUE--CONCLUSION

For a few moments after the collapse of the cave, and the destruction of the airship, on which they depended to take them from that desolate land, no one spoke. The calamity had been too terrible--they could hardly understand it.

The snow had ceased, and, over the frozen plain, in full retreat, could be seen the band of attacking Indians. They had fled in terror at the manifestation of Nature. And Nature, as if satisfied at the mischief she had wrought, called a halt to the movement of the ice. The roaring, grinding sounds ceased, and there were no more collapses of caves in that neighborhood.

"Well, we are up against it," spoke Tom, softly. "Poor old RED CLOUD! There'll never be another airship like you!"

"We are lucky to have escaped with our lives," said Mr. Parker. "Another moment and it would have been too late. I was expecting something like this--I predicted it."

But his honor was an empty one--no one cared to dispute it with him.

"Bless my refrigerator! What's to be done!" exclaimed Mr. Damon.

"Start from here as soon as possible," decided Abe.

"Why, do you think the natives will come back?" asked Ned.

"No, but we have only a small supply of food, my lad, an' it's hard to git up here. We must hit th' trail fer civilization as soon as we kin!"

"Go back--how; without the airship?" asked Tom, blankly.

"Walk!" exclaimed the miner, grimly. "It's th' only way!"

They realized that. There was no hope of digging through that mass of fantastically piled ice to reach the airship, and, even if they could have done so, it would have been crushed beyond all hope of repair. Nor could they dig down for more food, though what they had hastily saved was little enough.

"Well, if we've got to go, we'd better start," suggested Tom, sadly. "Poor old RED CLOUD!"

"Maybe we can get a little more gold," suggested Ned.

They walked over to the hole whence they had taken the yellow nuggets. The "pocket" was not to be seen. It was buried out of sight under tons of ice.

"We'll get no more gold here," decided Abe, "if we get safely out of th' valley, and t' the nearest white settlement, we'll be lucky."

"Bless my soul! Is it as bad as that!" cried Mr. Damon.

Abe nodded without speaking. There was nothing else to do. Sadly and silently they made up into packs the things they had saved, and started southward, guided by a small compass the miner had with him.

It was a melancholy party. Fortunately the weather had turned a little warmer or they might have been frozen to death. They tramped all that day, shaping their course to take them out of the valley on a side well away from where the hostile natives lived. At night they made rude shelters of snow and blocks of ice and ate cold victuals. The second day it grew colder, and they were slightly affected by snow-blindness, for they had lost their dark glasses in the cave.

Even the gold seemed too great a burden to carry, and they found they had more of it than at first they supposed. On the third day they were ready to give up, but Abe bravely urged them on. Toward the close of the fourth day, even the old miner was in despair, for the food they could carry was not such as to give strength and warmth, and they saw no game to shoot.

They were just getting ready to go into a cheerless camp for the night, when Tom, who was a little in advance, looked ahead.

"Ned, do I see something or is it only a vision?" he asked.

"What does it look like?" asked his chum.

"Like Eskimos on sleds."

"That's what it is," agreed Ned, after an observation. "Maybe it's the Fogers, or some of the savage Indians."

They halted in alarm, and got out their guns. The little party of natives kept coming on toward them.

Suddenly Abe uttered a cry, but it was one of joy and not fear.

"Hurrah!" he yelled, "It's all right--they're friendly natives! They're of the same tribe that helped me an' my partner! It's all right, boys, we're rescued now!"

And so it proved. A few minutes later the gold-seekers were on the sleds of the friendly Eskimos, some of whom remembered Abe, and the weary and hungry adventures were being rushed toward the native village as fast as the dogs could run. It was a hunting party that had come upon our friends just in time.

Little more remains to be told. Well cared for by the kind Eskimos, Tom and his friends soon recovered their spirits and strength. They arranged for dog teams to take them to Sitka, and paid their friends well for the service, not only in gold, but by presenting what was of more value, the guns they no longer needed. Tom, however, retained his electric rifle.

Three weeks after that they were on a steamer bound for civilization, having bidden their friends the Eskimos good-by.

"Homeward bound," remarked Tom, some time later, as they were in a train speeding across the continent. "It was a great trip, and the gold we got will more than repay us, even to building a new airship. Still, I can't help feeling sorry about the RED CLOUD."

"I don't blame you," returned Ned. "Are you going to build another airship, Tom?"

"Not one like the RED CLOUD, I think. But I have in mind plans for a sort of racing craft. I think I'll start it when I get back home."

How Tom's plans developed, and what sort of a craft he built will be related in the next volume of this series, to be called "Tom Swift and His Sky Racer; or, the Quickest Flight on Record." In that will be told how the young inventor foiled his enemies, and how he saved his father's life. Our friends arrived safely at Shopton in due season. They learned that the two Fogers had reached there shortly before them. Tom and his party decided not to prosecute them, and they did not learn the identity of the men who tried to rob Tom of the map.

"But I guess Andy won't go about boasting of his airship any more," said Ned, "nor of how he got our gold mine away from us. He'll sing mighty small for a while."

The store of gold brought from the North, proved quite valuable, though but for the unforeseen accidents our friends could have secured much more. Yet they were well satisfied. With his share Abe Abercrombie settled down out West, Mr. Damon gave most of his gold to his wife, Mr. Parker bought scientific instruments with his, Ned invested his in bank stock, and Tom Swift, after buying a beautiful gift for a certain pretty young lady, used part of the remainder to build his Sky Racer.

And now, for a time, we will take leave of Tom and his friends, and say good-by.

The Codes Of Hammurabi And Moses
W. W. Davies

QTY

The discovery of the Hammurabi Code is one of the greatest achievements of archaeology, and is of paramount interest, not only to the student of the Bible, but also to all those interested in ancient history...

Religion   **ISBN: *1-59462-338-4***   **Pages:132**
MSRP $12.95

The Theory of Moral Sentiments
Adam Smith

QTY

This work from 1749. contains original theories of conscience amd moral judgment and it is the foundation for systemof morals.

Philosophy ISBN: *1-59462-777-0*   **Pages:536**
MSRP $19.95

Jessica's First Prayer
Hesba Stretton

QTY

In a screened and secluded corner of one of the many railway-bridges which span the streets of London there could be seen a few years ago, from five o'clock every morning until half past eight, a tidily set-out coffee-stall, consisting of a trestle and board, upon which stood two large tin cans, with a small fire of charcoal burning under each so as to keep the coffee boiling during the early hours of the morning when the work-people were thronging into the city on their way to their daily toil...

Pages:84

Childrens   ISBN: *1-59462-373-2*   *MSRP $9.95*

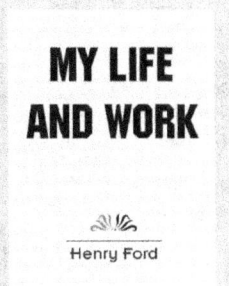

My Life and Work
Henry Ford

QTY

Henry Ford revolutionized the world with his implementation of mass production for the Model T automobile. Gain valuable business insight into his life and work with his own auto-biography... "We have only started on our development of our country we have not as yet, with all our talk of wonderful progress, done more than scratch the surface. The progress has been wonderful enough but..."

Pages:300

Biographies/   ISBN: *1-59462-198-5*   *MSRP $21.95*

The Art of Cross-Examination
Francis Wellman

QTY

I presume it is the experience of every author, after his first book is published upon an important subject, to be almost overwhelmed with a wealth of ideas and illustrations which could readily have been included in his book, and which to his own mind, at least, seem to make a second edition inevitable. Such certainly was the case with me; and when the first edition had reached its sixth impression in five months, I rejoiced to learn that it seemed to my publishers that the book had met with a sufficiently favorable reception to justify a second and considerably enlarged edition. ..

Reference   **ISBN:** *1-59462-647-2*

Pages:412

MSRP $19.95

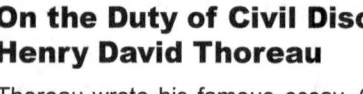

On the Duty of Civil Disobedience
Henry David Thoreau

QTY

Thoreau wrote his famous essay, On the Duty of Civil Disobedience, as a protest against an unjust but popular war and the immoral but popular institution of slave-owning. He did more than write—he declined to pay his taxes, and was hauled off to gaol in consequence. Who can say how much this refusal of his hastened the end of the war and of slavery ?

Law   **ISBN:** *1-59462-747-9*

Pages:48

MSRP $7.45

Dream Psychology Psychoanalysis for Beginners
Sigmund Freud

QTY

Sigmund Freud, born Sigismund Schlomo Freud (May 6, 1856 - September 23, 1939), was a Jewish-Austrian neurologist and psychiatrist who co-founded the psychoanalytic school of psychology. Freud is best known for his theories of the unconscious mind, especially involving the mechanism of repression; his redefinition of sexual desire as mobile and directed towards a wide variety of objects; and his therapeutic techniques, especially his understanding of transference in the therapeutic relationship and the presumed value of dreams as sources of insight into unconscious desires.

Psychology   **ISBN:** *1-59462-905-6*

Pages:196

MSRP $15.45

The Miracle of Right Thought
Orison Swett Marden

QTY

Believe with all of your heart that you will do what you were made to do. When the mind has once formed the habit of holding cheerful, happy, prosperous pictures, it will not be easy to form the opposite habit. It does not matter how improbable or how far away this realization may see, or how dark the prospects may be, if we visualize them as best we can, as vividly as possible, hold tenaciously to them and vigorously struggle to attain them, they will gradually become actualized, realized in the life. But a desire, a longing without endeavor, a yearning abandoned or held indifferently will vanish without realization.

Self Help   **ISBN:** *1-59462-644-8*

Pages:360

MSRP $25.45

www.bookjungle.com *email: sales@bookjungle.com fax: 630-214-0564 mail: Book Jungle PO Box 2226 Champaign, IL 61825*

QTY

The Rosicrucian Cosmo-Conception Mystic Christianity by *Max Heindel*   ISBN: *1-59462-188-8* **$38.95**
The Rosicrucian Cosmo-conception is not dogmatic, neither does it appeal to any other authority than the reason of the student. It is: not controversial, but is: sent forth in the, hope that it may help to clear...   New Age/Religion Pages 646

Abandonment To Divine Providence by *Jean-Pierre de Caussade*   ISBN: *1-59462-228-0* **$25.95**
"The Rev. Jean Pierre de Caussade was one of the most remarkable spiritual writers of the Society of Jesus in France in the 18th Century. His death took place at Toulouse in 1751. His works have gone through many editions and have been republished...   Inspirational/Religion Pages 400

Mental Chemistry by *Charles Haanel*   ISBN: *1-59462-192-6* **$23.95**
Mental Chemistry allows the change of material conditions by combining and appropriately utilizing the power of the mind. Much like applied chemistry creates something new and unique out of careful combinations of chemicals the mastery of mental chemistry...   New Age Pages 354

The Letters of Robert Browning and Elizabeth Barret Barrett 1845-1846 vol II   ISBN: *1-59462-193-4* **$35.95**
by *Robert Browning* and *Elizabeth Barrett*   Biographies Pages 596

Gleanings In Genesis (volume I) by *Arthur W. Pink*   ISBN: *1-59462-130-6* **$27.45**
Appropriately has Genesis been termed "the seed plot of the Bible" for in it we have, in germ form, almost all of the great doctrines which are afterwards fully developed in the books of Scripture which follow...   Religion/Inspirational Pages 420

The Master Key by *L. W. de Laurence*   ISBN: *1-59462-001-6* **$30.95**
In no branch of human knowledge has there been a more lively increase of the spirit of research during the past few years than in the study of Psychology, Concentration and Mental Discipline. The requests for authentic lessons in Thought Control, Mental Discipline and...   New Age/Business Pages 422

The Lesser Key Of Solomon Goetia by *L. W. de Laurence*   ISBN: *1-59462-092-X* **$9.95**
This translation of the first book of the "Lernegton" which is now for the first time made accessible to students of Talismanic Magic was done, after careful collation and edition, from numerous Ancient Manuscripts in Hebrew, Latin, and French...   New Age/Occult Pages 92

Rubaiyat Of Omar Khayyam by *Edward Fitzgerald*   ISBN:*1-59462-332-5* **$13.95**
Edward Fitzgerald, whom the world has already learned, in spite of his own efforts to remain within the shadow of anonymity, to look upon as one of the rarest poets of the century, was born at Bredfield, in Suffolk, on the 31st of March, 1809. He was the third son of John Purcell...   Music Pages 172

Ancient Law by *Henry Maine*   ISBN: *1-59462-128-4* **$29.95**
The chief object of the following pages is to indicate some of the earliest ideas of mankind, as they are reflected in Ancient Law, and to point out the relation of those ideas to modern thought.   Religion/History Pages 452

Far-Away Stories by *William J. Locke*   ISBN: *1-59462-129-2* **$19.45**
"Good wine needs no bush, but a collection of mixed vintages does. And this book is just such a collection. Some of the stories I do not want to remain buried for ever in the museum files of dead magazine-numbers an author's not unpardonable vanity..."   Fiction Pages 272

Life of David Crockett by *David Crockett*   ISBN: *1-59462-250-7* **$27.45**
"Colonel David Crockett was one of the most remarkable men of the times in which he lived. Born in humble life, but gifted with a strong will, an indomitable courage, and unremitting perseverance...   Biographies/New Age Pages 424

Lip-Reading by *Edward Nitchie*   ISBN: *1-59462-206-X* **$25.95**
Edward B. Nitchie, founder of the New York School for the Hard of Hearing, now the Nitchie School of Lip-Reading, Inc, wrote "LIP-READING Principles and Practice". The development and perfecting of this meritorious work on lip-reading was an undertaking...   How-to Pages 400

A Handbook of Suggestive Therapeutics, Applied Hypnotism, Psychic Science   ISBN: *1-59462-214-0* **$24.95**
by *Henry Munro*   Health/New Age/Health/Self-help Pages 376

A Doll's House: and Two Other Plays by *Henrik Ibsen*   ISBN: *1-59462-112-8* **$19.95**
Henrik Ibsen created this classic when in revolutionary 1848 Rome. Introducing some striking concepts in playwriting for the realist genre, this play has been studied the world over.   Fiction/Classics/Plays 308

The Light of Asia by *sir Edwin Arnold*   ISBN: *1-59462-204-3* **$13.95**
In this poetic masterpiece, Edwin Arnold describes the life and teachings of Buddha. The man who was to become known as Buddha to the world was born as Prince Gautama of India but he rejected the worldly riches and abandoned the reigns of power when...   Religion/History/Biographies Pages 170

The Complete Works of Guy de Maupassant by *Guy de Maupassant*   ISBN: *1-59462-157-8* **$16.95**
"For days and days, nights and nights, I had dreamed of that first kiss which was to consecrate our engagement, and I knew not on what spot I should put my lips..."   Fiction/Classics Pages 240

The Art of Cross-Examination by *Francis L. Wellman*   ISBN: *1-59462-309-0* **$26.95**
Written by a renowned trial lawyer, Wellman imparts his experience and uses case studies to explain how to use psychology to extract desired information through questioning.   How-to/Science/Reference Pages 408

Answered or Unanswered? by *Louisa Vaughan*   ISBN: *1-59462-248-5* **$10.95**
Miracles of Faith in China   Religion Pages 112

The Edinburgh Lectures on Mental Science (1909) by *Thomas*   ISBN: *1-59462-008-3* **$11.95**
This book contains the substance of a course of lectures recently given by the writer in the Queen Street Hall, Edinburgh. Its purpose is to indicate the Natural Principles governing the relation between Mental Action and Material Conditions...   New Age/Psychology Pages 148

Ayesha by *H. Rider Haggard*   ISBN: *1-59462-301-5* **$24.95**
Verily and indeed it is the unexpected that happens! Probably if there was one person upon the earth from whom the Editor of this, and of a certain previous history, did not expect to hear again...   Classics Pages 380

Ayala's Angel by *Anthony Trollope*   ISBN: *1-59462-352-X* **$29.95**
The two girls were both pretty, but Lucy who was twenty-one who supposed to be simple and comparatively unattractive, whereas Ayala was credited, as her Bombwhat romantic name might show, with poetic charm and a taste for romance. Ayala when her father died was nineteen...   Fiction Pages 484

The American Commonwealth by *James Bryce*   ISBN: *1-59462-286-8* **$34.45**
An interpretation of American democratic political theory. It examines political mechanics and society from the perspective of Scotsman James Bryce   Politics Pages 572

Stories of the Pilgrims by *Margaret P. Pumphrey*   ISBN: *1-59462-116-0* **$17.95**
This book explores pilgrims religious oppression in England as well as their escape to Holland and eventual crossing to America on the Mayflower, and their early days in New England...   History Pages 268

QTY

The Fasting Cure *by Sinclair Upton*   ISBN: *1-59462-222-1*   **$13.95**
In the Cosmopolitan Magazine for May, 1910, and in the Contemporary Review (London) for April, 1910, I published an article dealing with my experiences in fasting. I have written a great many magazine articles, but never one which attracted so much attention... New Age/Self Help/Health Pages 164

Hebrew Astrology *by Sepharial*   ISBN: *1-59462-308-2*   **$13.45**
In these days of advanced thinking it is a matter of common observation that we have left many of the old landmarks behind and that we are now pressing forward to greater heights and to a wider horizon than that which represented the mind-content of our progenitors... Astrology Pages 144

Thought Vibration or The Law of Attraction in the Thought World   ISBN: *1-59462-127-6*   **$12.95**
by William Walker Atkinson   *Psychology/Religion Pages 144*

Optimism *by Helen Keller*   ISBN: *1-59462-108-X*   **$15.95**
Helen Keller was blind, deaf, and mute since 19 months old, yet famously learned how to overcome these handicaps, communicate with the world, and spread her lectures promoting optimism. An inspiring read for everyone... Biographies/Inspirational Pages 84

Sara Crewe *by Frances Burnett*   ISBN: *1-59462-360-0*   **$9.45**
In the first place, Miss Minchin lived in London. Her home was a large, dull, tall one, in a large, dull square, where all the houses were alike, and all the sparrows were alike, and where all the door-knockers made the same heavy sound... Childrens/Classic Pages 88

The Autobiography of Benjamin Franklin *by Benjamin Franklin*   ISBN: *1-59462-135-7*   **$24.95**
The Autobiography of Benjamin Franklin has probably been more extensively read than any other American historical work, and no other book of its kind has had such ups and downs of fortune. Franklin lived for many years in England, where he was agent... Biographies/History Pages 332

Name	
Email	
Telephone	
Address	
City, State ZIP	

☐ **Credit Card**   ☐ **Check / Money Order**

Credit Card Number	
Expiration Date	
Signature	

Please Mail to: Book Jungle
                                    PO Box 2226
                                    Champaign, IL 61825
or Fax to: 630-214-0564

ORDERING INFORMATION

web*: www.bookjungle.com*
email*: sales@bookjungle.com*
fax*: 630-214-0564*
mail*: Book Jungle PO Box 2226 Champaign, IL 61825*
or PayPal *to sales@bookjungle.com*

Please contact us for bulk discounts

DIRECT-ORDER TERMS

**20% Discount if You Order
Two or More Books**
Free Domestic Shipping!
Accepted: Master Card, Visa,
Discover, American Express

www.ingramcontent.com/pod-product-compliance
Lightning Source LLC
Chambersburg PA
CBHW080746250626
47162CB00010B/3042